CHICK FLICK

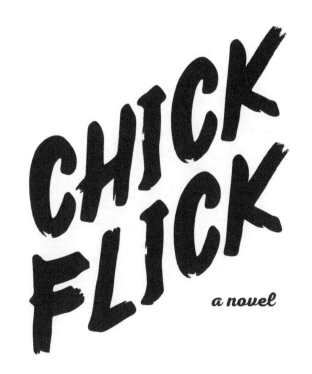

CHICK FLICK

a novel

NOGA PORAT

NEW YORK

NASHVILLE • MELBOURNE • VANCOUVER

CHICK FLICK

Published in New York, New York, by Morgan James Publishing. Morgan James is a trademark of Morgan James, LLC. www.MorganJamesPublishing.com

The Morgan James Speakers Group can bring authors to your live event. For more information or to book an event visit The Morgan James Speakers Group at www.TheMorganJamesSpeakersGroup.com.

ISBN 9781683504641 paperback
ISBN 9781683504658 eBook
Library of Congress Control Number: 2017902781

Cover and Interior Design by:
Chris Treccani
www.3dogcreative.ne

In an effort to support local communities, raise awareness and funds, Morgan James Publishing donates a percentage of all book sales for the life of each book to Habitat for Humanity Peninsula and Greater Williamsburg.

Get involved today! Visit
www.MorganJamesBuilds.com

"Where they burn books, at the end they also burn people"
Heinrich Heine, 1821

Certainly the same should be concluded about the senseless tossing away of billions of day-old male chicks

I dedicate this book to the memory of my beloved Father.

If only every girl in this world had a father like him, if only…

acknowledgments

I want to thank Sara Stratton for recognizing the potential of this endeavor and lighting the candle in my heart that burns for these injustices - a candle that almost blew out in the wind of life. For your experience and intelligence that allowed you this choice, I am forever grateful.

I want to thank J. from BusinessGhost, Inc for rummaging through my dresser drawer and making sense of my hidden work notes to illuminate the untold story of male chicks in the poultry industry. Your writing is impeccable, thrilling and inspiring.

I want to thank my mother for always standing by my side as I heal and walk through the journeys of pain. Life takes us by surprise, but your unwavering loyalty is not surprising, it is inherent in your character and the core strength of our bond. I love you, Mom!

You three women make all the hard work worthwhile.

For the rest of you who never invested but gave me good stories to tell, good laughs, good advice and good times...thanks for all the BS.

chapter 1

I t took me a long time to understand the importance of details. In my mind, when something was close, it was usually close enough.

Had I figured this out sooner, I might have been an engineer today—so close was my grade to the requirement for acceptance. Ironically, that fine detail, the two points I was missing from my score, was a detail I understood well enough. Those points would haunt me for a while, but the future had something else in mind for me.

Instead of engineering, I studied biology in school. Basic science is the business of acquiring knowledge; scientific research is like uncovering Mother Nature's secrets. I wanted more, though; I wanted to *create* things with the knowledge I acquired. Not content to be constrained by details, I preferred to use my imagination. It's a misconception that scientists aren't creative; we're just like any other artist, in fact. Our canvas is drastically different, but the strokes of our paint can achieve the same means.

I remember working on a project in the lab at school for my master's degree. A friend next door was working on a fascinating subject, exploring mechanisms to repair DNA. To simplify things, I liked to think of it as a *DNA spell-checker*. When DNA, the genetic material, is copied, errors are incorporated, just as spelling mistakes are incorporated when copying written information. The cell machinery repairs these mistakes by removing these "misspellings" and incorporating the correct "letters."

There was one factor of the cell machinery that I especially enjoyed: an enzyme—or in biological terms, a DNA "repair machine"—that could fix a specific "spelling mistake" all on its own. For instance, if every *c* is required to be a *k,* this amazing cellular machine would edit every *c* that needed to be corrected back to a *k.*

Unlike me, my father had an incredible eye for detail. Growing up, he paid particular attention while checking for spelling mistakes in my homework assignments. Each time I wrote a composition, he would take the time to sit with me, correcting my spelling and grammar. And this is why, when I learned that cells have a machine that functions similarly to my father, my first and best editor, I thought it was wonderful! Nothing expresses our thoughts, our creative inclinations, better than words, and spelling and grammar are what help make that communication clear.

Once I learned that cells have a "spell-checker," I felt compelled to understand it all, every last detail. This was a new feeling for me. I felt a tingle each time I found a new article on this subject. Little did I know how much this small, unique, elegant cellular machine would occupy my time and thoughts for the following ten years. I was so infatuated with this miraculous "spell-checker" enzyme that I had come up with ideas as to how to use it as a tool in biology, and even developed my own methods to use it in. In pursuit of my infatuation, I rented lab space, using my own seed money with the thought that if my research progressed, I could secure investments shortly thereafter.

Soon, I hit a wall; I needed real tissue samples to check my method of utilizing the "spell-checker" enzyme, rather than the synthetic DNA on which I'd been testing it. My friend Hayley was a biologist who rented space in the same lab complex, and I was talking to her when I discovered something that would eventually crack my world wide open.

"I'm at a dead end," I told her. "I need tissue samples."

"I know a company that uses chicken DNA as their study model," Hayley shared.

Not a bad idea, I thought, *and that won't require an approval from a Helsinki committee.* "What are they working on?"

I listened with rapt attention as Hayley explained that the company was working on trying to differentiate female from male chicks while the chicks were still in the egg, before they hatched. It wouldn't have occurred to me to see this as a problem that needed to be solved, until:

"It's horrible, you know. What happens to the newborn chicks."

I had to admit I didn't know.

"The poultry industry destroys newborn chicks left and right. It's not even an industry secret; it's just chalked up as the cost of doing business," she said.

What followed was a crash course in one of the facets of the world of poultry called the "layer industry." In the layer industry, the lives of male chicks had no value; only the females were needed to lay eggs. After hatching, male chicks are segregated and tossed into the garbage, completely without ceremony, usually in a dumpster behind the hatchery. All to the tune of two *billion* newborn chicks executed annually.

I had to know more. That night, I picked through the mess of my apartment and uncovered my computer. (My fastidiousness in the lab did not extend to my home! One of the perks of living alone, of course, is that it doesn't matter). I sat down and searched for more information, first making the unfortunate mistake of trying to Google "Chick Sexing" (don't do it!). After a few searches that were more finely tuned, I saw that the facts from Hayley's introductory lesson indeed bore out. It was amazing to me, in the most horrible sense, that in a world where we've put a man on the moon and you can have a morning meeting in Japan and an evening Skype with South Dakota, we are checking every single hatched chick by hand and destroying every male.

To help with the sexing process, the male and female laying chickens are genetically engineered to have different wing shapes. In the broiler industry—which produces chickens that we eat—separation isn't an issue. Thankfully, we eat both sexes of the broilers.

As horrified as I was by this new information, I was excited by the challenge too. The art of science is in solving problems, making things better. I had to research it further. I had so many questions. Why were they still separating them manually? Why not automatically, earlier, while still in the egg? What was the holdup? Was it scientifically challenging, or was it cheaper to preserve the status quo? I was sure it was scientifically possible, so maybe the poultry industry was way behind. Or maybe they just didn't care about the pain inflicted on these newborn chicks. Either way, I needed answers.

A farmer friend helped me obtain samples of blood from under the wing of both male and female chickens. Once I had real DNA to work on, I hurried back to the lab. I wanted to see if I could use the novel "spell-checker" method I had been developing to differentiate male and female DNA extracted from the chickens' blood. All of the sudden, I felt I had found the *killer application* for my method—though I don't mean that in the literal sense!

I had entered a zone; nourished by my work, I didn't feel the need to eat or sleep. I knew that if I could solve this problem, I'd be on my way to accomplishing an honorable and important goal, one that I could be proud of. Scientists set out to change the world not just because we can, but because we can make life better. I wanted to prevent pain inflicted on any life, fellow or fowl—no matter how small.

usiness wasn't my forte, but I knew enough to know that if I wanted my idea to change the world, or at least the layer industry, I would need to find some backers. Suddenly, I wasn't just talking about a scientific application; I was talking about a start-up. Reaching into my network for contacts, I found the name of a biotech guru, Dr. Eric Walters, who headed up Splice Incubator, a promising outfit that gave scientists a space to incubate start-ups and help them grow. I smiled to myself as I tapped out an e-mail to Dr. Walters; I'd need two kinds of incubators now, one for my research project and another for chicken eggs.

Incubators are essential to scientists and entrepreneurs who are working by themselves or with a small team. It's not often you'll have the resources to purchase a lab, not to mention all the administrative minutia you need to run an office. If you rent space in an incubator, you've got all kinds of resources at your fingertips, including advisors for financing, intellectual property, and on and on—all the things that one doesn't want to be bothered with when working on the bench in the lab. The downside? Someone has to pay for this stuff, obviously; that was part of the reason I needed investors.

First, though, I needed a partner. Todd Johnson was a good friend of mine who was just out of a start-up that had sold for a pretty penny. He was a numbers guy, mainly in the tech sector, with a background in computer science. He didn't know much about biotech, but I knew what I needed most was someone who could work magic at meetings with potential investors. He believed in the mission, and that was the first and most important point. Before I knew it, he'd crafted an incredibly persuasive business proposal just based on the little background I was able to help him absorb.

"It's not my first time at the rodeo, Scarlet," he'd said with a wink.

Clearly not.

Dr. Walters was impressed with the proposal, but we wanted to do our due diligence before we committed to signing on the dotted line with Splice. Todd was looking into meeting with a potential investor from the poultry industry. The investor, John Stanley, owned several hatcheries around the world, and was well aware of the problem we were aiming to fix. He seemed courteous and curious in his manner toward us, but I couldn't help but feel like he felt a head above us, as if he were there to give us an education rather than give us a chance to pitch him our business idea.

"I'm sure you're aware of the sheer size and financial clout of the poultry industry," he said, emphasizing the billions of dollars that changed hands around the layers and broilers each year.

This was accurate, and we certainly *were* well aware. Despite the gross financial product of the industry, it was still relatively small in scope; only four major corporations controlled the industry in the United States. Of these, the largest company, Avian Industrial, made $26 billion in the last year from egg-to-plate processing.

"These guys own this business," Stanley said. "From the farmer's hardworking hands all the way to the food on your breakfast plate. If you are going to sell this chick-sexing application, they are the people to impress. You really only have four customers."

Stanley was right, of course, but I hadn't thought about it in this way. Making four people happy didn't sound like it would be too hard; on the other hand, if those four hands shook against you, you were shut out for good.

"Is that a good or a bad thing?" I asked.

He smiled.

"Imagine the downside to dealing with a cartel," he said. I tried to hide my look of concern, but he was an experienced businessperson; he read me like an open book. "But, if you get their attention, you're off to a good start."

I felt hopeful, convinced that my idea was a great one, bound to capture the attention of the industry.

"I don't think we'll have a problem with that," I said confidently. "I'm an idealist. I believe that if we can produce a more humane solution to the problem, the industry will be all ears. It's a universal law that everyone prefers the moral high ground."

He chuckled.

"Listen. I know these guys. I've been at the table with them. They aren't easily impressed," he said. "I think what would really get their attention was if you could differentiate female from male eggs *in ovo* after only three days of incubation. What are your margins now?"

"Three days?" This was the first time Todd had piped up since the meeting had started. "We're nowhere near three days."

"It takes twenty-one days for an egg to hatch," I offered. "There's a larger window than just three days."

Again, Stanley cut me off. I couldn't tell if he really knew something we didn't, or if it was just his arrogance coming through. I thought that maybe he was underestimating me because I was a young woman. I sat up straighter, steeling myself for the patronizing lecture that might come.

"Scarlet, the moral issue may be important to you. But to the big four?" He made a motion like he was swatting away a fly. "You need more to get to them. If you can sex the chicks after three days of incubation, we can still sell them as eating eggs. We can make a profit on those male eggs."

"So this is about money?" I asked.

I didn't have the courage to look at Todd. I knew where he might come down on the issue; I'd convinced him of the moral importance of my project, but Todd was a businessperson first and foremost. I worried that he might be too easily swayed by talk of financial gain.

"Of course it is!" Stanley said, incredulous. "We are talking about peoples' livelihood, Scarlet, and if you try and mess with it, those industry people will get upset. They are used to their set ways. What am I going to do with the eggs if you sex them after three days? I can't sell those to moms to make breakfast with."

I shook my head. On this issue, I felt I could not budge.

"It's simply not possible to sex them before three days," I said. "The embryos don't even develop blood vessels until the *fourth* day. I need the blood vessels to draw the blood that I'll use to test the DNA."

"Well, I'm afraid I can't help you," he said, gathering his briefcase and standing up before Todd had another chance to open his mouth. "If I can't make a profit, sweetness, I can't do business."

s Todd and I walked through the city streets away from the meeting, my emotions ran the gamut from disappointment to anger to hope to disappointment again. It was summer in the city, and the steam rising from the asphalt seemed to mix with the steam coming from my ears.

Todd knew me well enough to know what was spinning through my mind.

"That guy's a jerk, Scarlet," he said. "He had no right to speak to you like that."

I looked to the sidewalk and watched tall, powerful men coming in and out of high buildings. I made a promise that I'd never let myself get so discouraged again that I would consider giving up on my dream; I don't want to prove the jerks of the world right. I gave him a quick pat on the shoulder to thank him and started walking faster. Surprised, he scrambled to catch up.

"Where are you off to now?"

I pulled out my phone and started thumbing through the contact list.

"I have an idea."

Todd loosened his tie, the sweat starting to soak through his collar as I walked faster and faster, nearly bowling into a food cart as I moved along the sidewalk.

"You seem to have a lot of those these days," he said.

I knew that we were down, but not out. If anything, the meeting with the potential investor had given me another puzzle to solve. In order to make our product attractive to outside capital, we had to figure out how to make a profit. We needed to make this about money after all—not because I believed in my moral cause any less, but because money was the key to attracting investors to help us realize the dream.

Hayley had given me a contact of an old friend of hers who had long ago made the leap from scientist to profiteer. Dean Albert worked for one of the processing plants that contracted to Avian Industrial, and he'd be the perfect person to help us do our homework on the ground level.

"It costs us one cent to separate each egg manually," Dean said as he offered us each a bottle of water and we split our attentions between the man behind the desk and the organized mayhem of the processing floor below. You could see it through large, spotless glass windows that overlooked the floor. "And we don't do the separation here. We buy them from the hatcheries already separated."

Being a former scientist, I found he was of a like mind when it came to solving problems and trying to better the world. He was kind, and I felt genuine relief and thankfulness as he went through the process with us, giving us all the facts and figures we needed without any spin. He eventually sent us back outside and out of the city limits, into a local hatchery that his processing plant worked with, so that we could see how the egg-separating process took place. I steeled myself; this wasn't going to be a happy thing for me to deal with.

All in the name of progress, I said to myself, squeezing my hands together in my lap on the way out to the hatchery.

Once we got outside of the city limits, the car felt more claustrophobic, not less. Perhaps this was because we weren't on our way to an idyllic barn, but rather, a major cog in the machine that is the poultry industry. The plant loomed cold and gray in front of us as we slid into a visitor's spot and began to go through the security process before we were allowed inside. Dean had called in advance of our coming, but there were still many papers to sign, liability waiver forms to initial, that kind of thing.

The hatchery is a sterile place. As a doctor would scrub in before surgery, Todd and I were instructed to wear protective clothing—not for our benefit, but for the benefit of the product—donning a sterile hat, gown, and mask. They would take no risk of contaminating the thousands of eggs they had in incubation. Kept at a perfect thirty-seven degrees Celsius, the incubator rooms are nice and warm; it would have been a treat on a cold winter day, but in the summer, it felt like we were overdressed and lying on a beach. In the sea of egg trays, one thing struck me as odd. Our guide had mentioned there being thousands of eggs in incubation, but were there even a thousand eggs in this room? Would I even know a thousand eggs if I saw them? I started to count, doing the math while Todd talked to the hatchery worker.

"Is this it?" I interrupted, not one for patience when it came to my projects.

"Oh no," the worker said, and I thought I saw the corners of his mask perk up as if he were smiling. The incubator is designed like the inside of a spiral shell. We're only in one part of it."

We followed him to another room, where eggs at eighteen days of incubation were injected with vaccines. The room was cavernous, with a huge machine that accepts the egg trays loaded by conveyer belt and pulled gently into rubber suction cups. These cups register the inside volume of each egg, checking first if there's an embryo inside. An egg without an embryo will be cold, owing to its lack of life. There's no need to waste a vaccine on an empty egg.

Once the fertilization status is marked, a long arm goes through and pulls each unfertilized egg out of the tray and onto a metal trough in the side. Each egg cracks with the pressure of the cold metal—imagine hundreds of sunny-side-up eggs waiting to be fried. These are waste products, of course.

With the waste separated, tiny needles are pushed down into the suction cups holding the fertilized eggs, silently puncturing the shell. I'd seen this before, but Todd hadn't; he was amazed that the shells didn't crack.

Our guide had seen that look of amazement before.

"Pretty cool, huh? The chicks turn out perfectly fine. In the '90s, RICPCom successfully built a machine that could provide inoculation against common diseases *in ovo*. They are the only ones who tried to do it in the egg," he said. "Their plant is here in town, actually. They come out and do all the maintenance and support. It's a closed system, and they keep a pretty tight lock on it, but it's a bunch of friendly guys."

"Before they came up with that machine, was the inoculation done manually?" I wondered aloud.

"Yup. What a pain, right?" He slapped his knee with the clipboard he was holding. "This is way better. They used to inoculate them as they were hatched, one by one. Now it's efficient, and saves the handling of the chicks. Once the egg is in the suction cup in the proper position, the needle is calibrated to inject it in the shoulder. Or what passes for a shoulder of an embryo, anyway."

He led us into another large room.

"It would be great if someone could figure out a better way to deal with this," he grumbled.

I knew instantly we were in the sorting room. On seven high chairs, seven women sat with gloves and covered heads as they separated out chicks, one per second, thirty-six hundred an hour. The chicks fall out of the shoot, and then make their way from the hatching trays to the round platform where they are circled, until they are picked up and segregated. Once the worker determines the sex, the male is thrown into another shoot, sliding along the cold platform onto the conveyer belts into baskets to be tossed away outside into the hatchery garbage. The females slide into baskets, which are taken to farms to grow and lay eggs. One for life, the other for death. I had to look away, and I saw Todd beginning to viscerally understand why this issue was so important to me. The males suffocate one on top of one another outside in the dumpster.

At last, we were shown the hatching room, another warm room with eggs held together in baskets. It was like a bright Saturday-morning cartoon, watching the eggs rub against each other as they lightly hopped in place, hatching. It's amazing to watch a little chick hatch, immediately standing on his own two feet as his brothers and sisters pop out of the eggs around him. If you look closely, you can even see them try to fly a little. Thousands of small, downy, yellow-feathered chicks appearing before my eyes out of a sea of whiteness—they were so adorable, I wanted to hug each and every one of them, or at the very least, give them a pet on the soft spot just above their beak between the eyes. I couldn't help but coo a little, and I blushed when I saw that the hatchery worker had heard me.

After we left the hatchery, Todd told me that now he understood more about the process, including the profit, but more important, my objections to the industry's standard practices.

"We can do this, Scarlet," he said, excitedly waving his notepad around as we walked back to the car. It was closing in on dusk, and the summer heat was blessedly abating. "If we manage to automate this process, we can absolutely do it in a profitable way."

In any case, we were certainly more prepared to meet our next investor, avoiding the embarrassment we'd felt earlier. I had more to learn on the biotechnology end; I needed to know who else had tried to solve this issue and what stumbling blocks they'd run into. Before we left the hatchery, our guide was telling us about some of the inside information he had on other companies trying to develop techniques for their own sexing applications, but to no avail.

"If there was a machine for that, believe me, we'd know about it. We'd have a couple right here in the hatchery," he said.

chapter 4

"It's time to get started, Scarlet," said Todd one day. "We can do this thing!"

I felt the familiar tug of self-doubt inside me. I had been working on my own for so long; I knew that we needed to get going, but somewhere I still hadn't accepted that we were going to take this leap. Turning a dream into a reality is frightening!

But more than my fear, the excitement started to take over. I didn't want to be one of those young scientists who got stuck in the fear of the unknown, freezing in my tracks and not trying. I knew then that the fear was part and parcel of this excitement, a feeling that I wouldn't trade for any other, because that feeling came with HOPE. I would rather have hope, strive to achieve my dream, and fall on my face later rather than never having hope at all and never doing anything to make things better.

So we took the plunge. We went downtown to a sleek high-rise, where a tall, elegantly dressed woman showed us to another conference room, this time, with a friendlier air.

"Would you like something to drink? Coffee? Water?"

We shook our heads. We were too nervous to hold anything.

"OK," she said, then smiled. "Lauralynn will be right in to see you."

We took in the view of the city as we waited for Lauralynn Franklin, the woman we hoped would be our lawyer. She had come highly recommended, and after that first disastrous meeting, we knew our nascent operation needed legal protection. We owed that first great idea that much. The drop from the fifty-seventh floor was precipitous, but from our seats at the conference table, all we could see was beautiful clear blue sky. The feeling of possibility opened up before us. Looking out the windowed walls, I tried to catch my breath; I knew this was a rare moment, one to be valued. My head spun and I sat back down.

When Lauralynn walked in with a smile, I felt immediately at ease. A petite woman with a big heart, which she clearly wore on her sleeve, she wasn't at all what I had pictured. I've read my share of nail-biting crime thrillers, and lawyers always seem like wolves, emissaries of corporate greed. I could tell instantly that Lauralynn wasn't like that. She was sharp, indeed, but with a straightforward, no-nonsense approach. I liked her immediately. I never thought she was trying to take advantage of us, even though she could probably see we were wet behind the ears.

"It's such a pleasure to meet you both," she said, sitting not across the expanse of the glassy table, but right next to us, angling her chair toward us. "I was so interested when I read your prospectus. Tell me more about this idea of yours."

Normally, I might have let Todd do the talking, but something about Lauralynn put me at ease. I felt like she could be a mentor, a role model.

"We're developing a novel technique to differentiate between male and female chicks *in ovo*," I said. "While still in the egg, that is."

She nodded, and listened intently as I went on with my explanation. I told her about the barbaric practices of the layer industry, what happened to the male chicks, and how I thought I could come up with a better solution. I appreciated that she was so interested; it wasn't her job to fund the endeavor, and she could simply draw up the papers and take our money no matter what. But I could tell she really cared about what we were trying to do.

"And the shares in the company—you're planning to divide them fifty-fifty between you two?"

"Yes," replied Todd and I simultaneously.

I could feel my heart beating in my throat. Signing papers. Starting a company. This was huge for a young scientist. It felt like something only "grown-ups" would do, people like those whom I'd spent my career so far working under. To work on a bench is one thing, but to sign contracts? To state publicly that I had something worth pursuing, worth giving to the world? That was a whole different ball of wax.

Unlike the men and women we'd encountered so far on our journey, Lauralynn wasn't sarcastic or hard-edged. She was respectful, curious and genuine. Just when I thought it couldn't get any better, she made us an offer we couldn't refuse.

"I think I can help you," she said. "Not only that, but I think I can help you without any money changing hands."

A little laugh escaped Todd's lips; I self-consciously tried to rearrange my features into something less reminiscent of a grimace.

"I'm not pulling your leg," she continued. "I love this project, and I'm fortunate enough to be in a successful practice with a diverse array of clients. I can afford to help you pro bono for now, with the expectation that when you get investors on board, we can settle up our accounts."

Lauralynn's belief in us floored me. More than that, it reassured me. Maybe this idea was as great as I'd thought. Maybe, as I would be fighting for this step by step, I wouldn't have to do it alone. I would have people like Todd and Lauralynn on my side, for starters. After all, my friends hadn't laughed when I told them about the start-up. I looked out at the blue sky surrounding us and felt, for a moment, on top of the world.

"You'll need more than just me to get this done, though," she said.

I started scribbling furiously on my notepad. Ever the eager student, I wasn't going to pass up this education in opening our business.

"You'll need an accountant to go over the bills and help you prepare your tax forms. I can handle the registration of the company and any dealings you may have with potential investors or buyers, but we need to make sure the finances are in order," she said, adding with a wink, "when there *are* finances, that is."

Todd nodded. We spent some time talking about the organizational structure, with Todd as the CEO and me as the CTO—chief technical officer. Of course, that meant I was also the researcher, the lab technician, the one to send the invoices, the one who made the coffee, and the one buying the sandwiches for lunch. It was a busy job, but someone had to do it . . . and I had to eat! The point being, it was a small operation.

Lauralynn seemed to think this all made sense. "And what's the name going to be?"

"Spells," I said, proudly. It was the "spell-checking" enzyme, after all, that had inspired me, and ever since then, I'd felt like a spell had been cast over me, running through my thoughts nonstop.

The rest of the meeting passed by in a blur of paperwork and excitement. At the end of it all, it was official: Todd and I had opened our own company.

But there would be little time to celebrate just yet.

chapter 5

Even though it was getting late, I couldn't wait to get back to the lab, throw on my coat, and dive into the research. I had to dig deeper into the literature. Todd had a different idea. He sounded as sure of this as I'd ever heard him sound about any idea.

"Scarlet," he said. "It's time we contacted RICPCom."

The more cautious of the two of us, I felt my resolve start to shake. RICPCom was not just a major player in the business, they were a potential competitor, one of the two companies we knew of that were working on applications for automatic chick separation. It was a natural pipeline product for them, of course, since they owned the patents for injecting into the egg. It followed that at the time the needle entered for the inoculation, you could draw a sample to sex the chick.

"You're nuts," I said, trying to laugh off my visible stress. "We're not ready for that!"

"Scarlet, I know you like to look before you leap. I totally understand that," Todd said, gently trying to talk me down. "We've got to do this now. They are potential collaborators, or customers, at the very least. And it takes time to develop a business relationship!"

I think he could tell right away that I wasn't convinced, because later that day, he disappeared from the office for a while, serendipitously contacting RICPCom reps from his car . . . or trying to, anyway. They were harder to get ahold of than one might assume about a relatively small company. After he'd been told that the CEO was out of the country, he was connected to Caroline Peters, the CTO. After haggling with her for a few minutes of her time, he was able to secure a time for us to connect with her and her chief researcher. I have to credit Todd's ingenuity with getting in touch with her at all; as simple as it is to pick up a phone and call rather than send an e-mail to solicit meetings, nobody thinks to do it anymore. And, after all, it's harder to say no on the phone.

Typical Todd, miracle worker. Despite the fact that he only had a couple minutes with her on the phone, he managed to give her a clear and compelling pitch about what we were working on. No doubt he got her attention by mentioning that our application would add value to their already valuable injection device.

"She pushed back a little bit," Todd admitted, "hinting that they were working on their own stuff, of course, and that they would have a conflict of interest. But I convinced her to hear us out when I told her our application was based on DNA, rather than simply hormones."

"Accuracy equals potential profits, right?"

"Exactly. You're getting the hang of this money thing," he said playfully.

Even though we were just set up for a conference call rather than a sit-down meeting, I still felt a lump forming in my throat. When I was on my bench day in and day out, doing my work, it seemed only a pipe dream that I'd be talking to someone so important as Caroline, someone who supervises the research and development (R&D) team of a company, where a groundbreaking product such as the *in ovo* inoculator was invented. What would someone with her degree of responsibility and experience say about our little project? Our venture seemed so small by comparison. But it was ours nevertheless, and we truly believed in it. To prepare for the call, I studied relentlessly as if I were working toward taking the Bar Exam. Late at night, lying in bed unable to sleep, I tried to anticipate questions and the answers I might give. There was so much at stake, and it felt like we were newly hatched, pun very much intended.

We didn't want anyone overhearing us in the lab, and we didn't want to bother Lauralynn again; she'd already given us so much and asked for nothing in return. So we did what scrappy, tiny start-ups did, and we worked with what we had. Which was, in this case, the interior of Todd's family sedan. I was stretched out in the back, he, in the front. I traced my fingers over the bright stickers that his four kids had stuck to the windows and clenched my teeth with something like anticipation and dread, waiting for the line to connect.

The dial tone terminated, and then came the telltale click of a speakerphone being activated somewhere far away. An authoritative voice rang out clearly, surrounding us through Todd's car speakers.

"Caroline Peters."

"Caroline!" Todd said with steely bravado, doing a wonderful acting job. It was like they were old buddies from business dealings past. "How's everything on your end?"

"It's fine," came the curt reply.

"Thank you so much for taking the time to talk to us," he continued. "I'm here with the brains of the operation, Scarlet."

He threw a teething toy into the back of the car, trying to wake me from my reverie. My voice sounded like it was coming out of a pillow of down, the thick fog of sleep.

"Hello, Ms. Peters," I croaked.

"Caroline," she said, and I reached to find the warmth in her tone. It felt like it was there somewhere, maybe just lost in translation over the phone lines. As she spoke more, a kindness began to emerge. "I'm here with Nikola Podgursky, my principal research-and-development gal. I don't take any calls on potential products without her blessing."

"Totally understand," said Todd. "Scarlet is my right hand here. And honestly, probably my left."

I listened in rapt attention at how Todd manipulated the situation: talking me up, knowing I'd be the one doing most of the explaining.

"As you're probably aware," Caroline said, "We've been developing our own sexing application using hormones. Nikola and her team have been hard at work on that project for some time now. But Todd's pitch was interesting, and we wanted to hear more about the proprietary technology you guys have cooking. 'Spells,' is it?"

"That's right, Caroline," Todd said. "Spelled like it sounds."

I groaned inside, and tossed the teething toy back at Todd. He smiled at me in the rearview mirror, already more at ease.

I cleared my throat, trying to rid it of the nervous croak I'd taken on before.

"Nice to meet you both," I began. "We're developing a proprietary assay for chick sexing by extracting DNA from the egg and examining it outside of the egg on a platform. This aligns with your intent with the hormone solution, but this is a more reliable and novel approach because genetics does not lie."

I hoped that I wasn't insulting Nikola, a fellow scientist. I didn't doubt she'd put in many hours working on her application.

"We've already developed a framework for the tests," said Nikola, a firmness in her voice, but obliging nonetheless. "We've made a fair amount of progress designing custom plates that will fit into a reading machine retrofitted to the injection machine. The robotic arm should swing seamlessly back and forth between inoculation and the reading plate."

"Well," said Todd, "I think this still sounds like it could be a wonderful partnership. Seamless, as you say. Scarlet can explain now."

"Nikola, what we're hoping is that we can provide the biological reaction that performs the identification of the sex, and that RICPCom can provide the logistical technology for extracting the sample from the egg and placing it onto the reading platform for examination. So in this respect, we would like to integrate our product into your production line, and that is why we initiated contact."

There was a brief silence before Caroline responded. I assumed they were speaking to one another out of range of the handset.

"I see what you're after," said Caroline.

"I do have a few questions, though, if you wouldn't mind indulging me," I ventured.

"Go ahead," said Nikola.

"I'm wondering if it's possible to extract a drop of blood while the needle goes in for vaccination without hurting the chick."

Nikola responded immediately, and I could feel the pride in her creation.

"Absolutely," she said. "When the needle is inserted, the angle is set to inject the chick on the shoulder. That region has many blood vessels, so there is usually a tiny drop of blood when the needle exits the egg. This can be placed on the test plate for processing."

Caroline chimed in. "I believe it also has residual scrapes of skin material. Would that help serve your purpose?"

With every minute, I was becoming braver. I could tell that they were taking us seriously. My pipe dream seemed so much more real, so much more within reach.

"Absolutely," I said. "Can I ask, what have been your challenges to getting the sample from the egg onto the reading platform?"

"It's an issue of scale. Can you hear me rolling my eyes over here?" said Caroline, and Todd and I laughed. We could relate to the frustration. "Imagine an egg tray of a certain size, set to hold a certain amount of eggs. Let's say, for argument's sake, one hundred eggs. Now, think of each needle over each egg transferring the sample from the egg to a correlating place on a reading plate. The current state-of-the-art reading equipment is manufactured for small plates, not the size of large egg trays, so there is a difference-of-dimensions problem."

"Got it," Todd and I said in unison.

"In order to transfer the sample from the egg to the fluorescent reader, you need to either solve the transfer problem of the robotic arms or build a new detection machine, made specifically for this purpose. Which costs money, of course," explained Nikola. "On top of that, we also have different-sized egg trays because of variable requirements from the different hatcheries. There's no standard egg-size tray, so this is all hard to translate."

"Wow," I said. "I thought I had a problem with designing the reaction to work under the hatchery restrictions. I wasn't even thinking about equipment details."

"Well, that, and of course, the time limit and cost requirements," said Caroline. "We need to get all the costs down in order to be efficient and profitable. But that's a discussion for another time."

I blushed on the other end of the line. Of course I was getting ahead of myself.

"You're right, obviously," I conceded. "We do need to finish our proof of concept."

"But we simply couldn't wait to talk to you," said Todd. "You are absolutely the leader in this field, and we needed to introduce ourselves, even at this early stage. We hope to reach our first milestone within the year, and we wanted to give RICPCom first shot at what we come up with."

Todd gave a cursory glance in the rearview mirror to make sure that I was OK with what he was spinning, but I had become distracted by the cars driving down the street. It had started to rain, and the water traced calming, organic patterns down the windows, erased by the occasional splash from a passing motorcycle.

"Understood," said Caroline. "We're always on the lookout for good ideas, especially if those ideas integrate with us directly."

We chatted for a while longer, Nikola and I throwing theories back and forth of what could be accomplished. What if, she suggested, we could somehow distinguish eggs with male DNA with a luminescent green color viewable through the shell. Our assay was currently intended for external examination only, so it didn't hurt to think about this pie-in-the-sky kind of stuff. I was in awe of Nikola; *I want to be like her when I grow up,* I thought to myself with a smile.

Todd broke in on the nerdy reverie we'd spun around ourselves.

"Caroline, what have you heard about this company out in France, NavoLogic?"

Caroline was taken aback; you could tell that wasn't something that happened to her often.

"Excuse me?"

"I don't know much about them, but I do know they're working on an application that can be used internally. They might not be too far off from those green eggs. I'm not sure," Todd said.

I was worried that Caroline and Nikola would take this as us trying to make a power play, trying to knock them down a peg. But it quickly became clear that they knew that wasn't the case. It was as though they trusted us already, even though we hadn't entered into any agreement, informal or otherwise.

"Impossible," Nikola said.

"Well, you're right about that," I jumped in. I had spent some time scouring the literature in my last cram session before the call. There were hints here and there, nothing too formed, but there was something that couldn't be ignored happening across the Atlantic. "It's actually an ultrasound technology," I said. "They want to be able to listen to the heartbeat of the chick and determine the sex from that. Apparently the male chicks' hearts beat faster." *It's ironic,* I thought. *Almost like they're nervous about their grisly future.*

Caroline had composed herself while I'd continued.

"I know NavoLogic, but I had no idea they were working on this," she said.

Later that night, I kept turning over in my mind the end of our conversation. It had been a success, and we had arranged for a follow-up meeting with Caroline and Nikola once we were a little further along. But the fact that Caroline, CTO of such an influential company in the business, didn't know what NavoLogic was up to felt wrong to me. Either she was keeping secrets from us—which didn't seem likely— or NavoLogic and its investors were working very, very hard to keep secrets from her. The questions hung in the air with the moon outside my window.

chapter 6

After business hours for most people were over, I got a call from Todd asking me to meet him at a nearby pub. He wanted to go over the conference call with RICPCom and talk strategy. We usually met for lunch, in the staid light of day, but I had spent so long cooped up in the lab that I had to admit, a nice, relaxing beverage with my business talk would suit me quite nicely.

"I could use a drink," I admitted. "I'm so relieved to be done with that call, and the fact that they didn't ridicule us for being so early on in the research phase. We should celebrate."

"That's my girl," said Todd, and he gave me the address for the Flying Cow. It was in a part of town I hadn't been to before, deep downtown where the streets were usually buzzing with bankers. Except for people like us, on their way to grab a happy-hour special, it was quiet.

I walked into the Flying Cow, appraising its warm, worn wood and the pleasantly yeasty smell of the beer. Oh, how I needed a beer! I sat down at the bar and ordered a tall, cool glass of Carlsberg while I waited for Todd. The bartender sat a small plate of nuts down in front of me, and I munched while people-watching. There were couples on dates, lone construction foremen nursing pints and pitchers, even a young family spoon-feeding mashed potatoes to a round little cherub.

It had been so long since I'd been to a bar; I couldn't even remember the last time I had a drink, let alone a night out. I let myself exhale in a deep sigh and slump into the bar a little, the beer warming my belly. How different this place was from my usual haunt, the lab, where I would stay late into the night taking advantage of the quiet after all my lab mates had gone home to their families. I could always hear myself think best at night. Sometimes, even if I'm not working on anything in particular, just sitting on my bench and staring at a blank wall for an hour would ignite a chain of thought and I could see things as clear as day.

But tonight was different. Other than talking strategy with Todd, I didn't want to do much thinking. I wanted simply to have a drink, relax a little, and feel a part of the world. I didn't even think I would shoulder too much of the strategic burden in our conversation, knowing that I'd leave most of the heavy lifting in that area to Todd. *I am the brains of the operation,* I thought with a smile. *I don't need to be the business mind.*

More important to our partnership, I was willing to be a good listener. When Todd and I formed our partnership, he let me know that his one condition was that he wouldn't have to be a yes-man. I agreed with him immediately, of course, and always made an effort to hear his opinion, even if I didn't necessarily agree at first. I let him know his opinion mattered to me, and that *he* mattered to me, and he extended me the exact same courtesy.

I could start to feel a pleasant buzz from the beer, and I began to gently ruminate on the nature of success in business. It wasn't something I'd put much thought into before this venture, and it could be stressful for me at times—*most* times, if I was being honest with myself. Our conference call with RICPCom definitely constituted success, I thought. Whereas I would have ordinarily thought of success only in terms of sales, Todd taught me that salesmanship was about more than just the sale itself. It was about following the idea every step of the way, watching every fork in the road and carefully mapping which turn to take.

Start-ups were particularly tricky, at least from what I could tell. There were so many people we had to put our trust in: the lawyer, VCs, other industry partners. When I thought about it too much, sometimes I got a little paranoid, thinking that there wasn't much of a point to my work if all that was going to happen in the end was that other people were going to profit big and sell my ideas. But this was something that I believed in, and furthermore, I had put my trust in Todd to drive us down the right path. And tonight, we weren't in the lab, so I'd be relying on him to take the wheel.

I was zoning out and watching the misspelled closed-captions on the newscast roll across the screen of the muted TV when I felt a tap on my shoulder. Todd's hair was windblown, and he loosened his tie a bit as he sat down, sighing.

"Man, I'm beat. I am officially done with meetings!" he said.

"It's a good thing we're not having a meeting," I said, smiling.

"Darn right."

He flagged over the bartender.

"I'll have what she's having. It looks delicious." Then, as if to show that he meant it quite ravenously, he scooped up the last of my salted nuts and tossed them back into his mouth. "And another bowl of these guys, please. Oh, and if you have those green olives, I will have a bowl of those as well. Thanks."

"Busy day?" I asked.

"Yeah. I try to keep focused on the job when I'm at the office. I wish I could be with you in the lab, watching you work!"

"It's better this way," I said. "Besides, you have a family to provide for. Until we find a major investor, looks like you'll need to keep your day job."

"If you say so, Scar," he said, sighing dramatically.

After Todd's beer arrived and his blood sugar leveled out a little bit from the nuts, we segued into talking about the conference call.

"I didn't know you knew so much about what NavoLogic was up to," he said.

"Sorry," I said, "I really went on a deep dive into the literature the night before the call. I was so nervous, I couldn't sleep."

"Where'd you find that info?"

"It's hidden, but it's there. And people in biotech talk. I was surprised she didn't know about it, though. Weren't you?"

"I was. It seems like she's an influencer in the industry."

"So something's definitely up with keeping that siloed."

"I mean, if NavoLogic get their hands on that kind of separation technology, they will own this market," I said. "They've got everything you need for the broiler, layer, and turkey hatcheries, and if they get their hands on chick sexing too, they will have nailed it!"

Todd nodded. "I'm glad we told her then. It's a strategic advantage almost."

"I didn't intend it that way, but I see that it is. She likes us for trading that information. Right now, RICPCom is a one-product company: their injection machine, which can inject vaccinations into the egg. It's their main source of revenue, and the patents are about to expire on that technology! They desperately need a new product to run through that machine and that's where the sexing application comes in," I said. "NavoLogic, on the other hand, sells hatchery equipment, so they are not dependent on the chick sexing because no one will bite into their profits if they don't produce it. But RICPCom's competitors are waiting on the sidelines to dig into their inoculation profits once the patents expire. If they want to hold on to their customer base and maintain exclusiveness in the field, they need us. We can deliver on the sexing application where they have failed."

I could see the wheels spinning in Todd's brain.

"We can use this to our advantage," he responded.

"More than we already are?"

"Yeah. I'm thinking, we contact NavoLogic. If we get more than one offer for our technology, we can start a bidding war," he said.

I started to bristle at the idea, draining the rest of my beer down to the suds. I didn't want to feel like I was betraying Caroline's confidence. She agreed to share technology information with us freely. But in reality, I knew what Todd would say: *We're not here to make friends.*

"I'm not talking about anything nefarious," Todd said. "We're just going to make it clear to them that we have access to important information. We're not going to talk about the content."

As I promised Todd, I listened. But I wasn't done digesting what he'd said, and I wasn't totally sure that I agreed.

"Just think about it, Scarlet," he said. "This could be big for us."

"OK. I'm going to keep my promise."

"That's right. No yes-men here," he said.

"Or yes-women," I pointed out.

"Right. No yes-people. Only possibility-people," he said.

"I like that."

Todd thought out loud for a little while, walking through the possibilities. He thought it would be great if there was a way to leak through the grapevine the notion that we had important information. I was more interested in getting back into the hatchery to learn more about the process. My mind was traveling in a different direction, back to the order and test tubes of the lab, the environment that I knew best and loved. Todd was still on the path to parlaying information to our advantage.

"NavoLogic doesn't have an injection device," he pointed out. "So they might be more flexible. Then again, it's a disadvantage, because it would take time for them to develop their own technology."

Back in the recesses of my brain, something pinged in the dark. I remembered some gossip I had heard in the industry.

"Not necessarily," I said. Todd's eyes glinted, and he leaned closer. "There's another company in the mix. They're small, but they have already developed a prototype for a competing injection machine. They're even poking fun at them about the name; they call their machine InjectEgg, a slight variation on RICPCom's machine."

"Aha, good Watson," said Todd with a smirk. "So *that's* why whichever company gets their hands on a chick-sexing application first will be the winner. Because there are already two types of injection machines."

"Yes, Todd, the expiration of RICPCom's patents is their Achilles' heel. The sexing application is the only way to add value to RICPCom's injection technology," I said, raising my glass to Todd's. The bartender had come and swapped out a full beer for my empty glass.

Todd clinked my glass.

"Here's to getting our technology in the works. I am starting to see how we can spin all of this to our advantage."

"Spin away, Todd."

chapter 7

We sat at the bar for a little longer, happy to relax together in the glow of our nascent plans and the warm lights hanging above us. Todd, checking his watch, started to gather his things.

"I gotta get home," he said. "Already missed the kids' bedtime. That's a big no-no in our house!"

He apologized and left despite my saying I wanted to stay a little longer. *I never have a night away from the lab,* I thought, *might as well make the most of it.* I traced my fingers along the bar, daydreaming about all the amazing opportunities that could open up for us if our application became the bargaining chip in what had the potential to become a very expensive battle between major players in the poultry industry.

A hand rapping on the bar next to me broke me out of my reverie. I turned to see a handsome stranger on the stool next to me, leaning in closer as he made a play for my attention. His eyes hummed with electricity, a cool green in the low light of the bar.

"I couldn't help but overhear some of your conversation," he said.

I tried to balance my competing emotions: anger at him for snooping and bashfulness as a result of his handsome visage. I wanted to immediately crawl away and out the door back to the safety of my lab when I spat out a reply that hedged too much into the realm of the self-defensive and sarcastic.

"I'm sure you could have, actually," I said.

To my surprise, and relief, he laughed, not so much with his mouth but more with his eyes.

"That's fair enough," he said, nodding and extending his hand. "I'm William."

I extended my hand to shake his. It was warm, dry, and confident. I hoped mine wasn't too clammy.

"Scarlet Struck," I said.

"It's nice to meet you, Scarlet."

I paused, encouraged by his friendliness and my pleasant evening buzz. He seemed harmless enough, even though the hard line of his jaw was drawing my attention. I blushed.

"So, since it was my conversation you were so interested in, do you mind sharing what it was that you overheard?"

"Oh, you know. Chicken things," he said with a wink.

"Do you have anything to do with them?"

He paused thoughtfully.

"I try not to overdo it," he said. "Cholesterol and all that. But I mean, who can resist a good omelet?"

I blinked and stared blankly. *What a beautiful, strong voice*, I thought. I must have looked peeved, because he quickly rushed to correct any ill impressions. He put his hand on my shoulder and my heart spiked into an arrhythmia.

"I'm sorry," he said. "That was in poor taste. I'm a journalist, sort of. A blogger, I guess. Internet only."

I nodded encouragingly. "That's not a bad thing."

"Well, I'd prefer to be pounding the pavement and returning at the end of my beat to an old-fashioned newsroom," he said with a smile. "I'm an old-fashioned kind of guy. In any case, I couldn't help but hear you and your business partner talking about some technology you're developing. Can't break the habit, stories are all around me."

"So that's how you get your stories? Eavesdropping?"

He shrugged. "I always assume that if a conversation is truly private, it would be held behind closed doors," he said.

"That assumption is a mistake."

"Maybe." Another devilish smile. "Maybe your assumption of privacy is *your* mistake, though."

I assessed the situation, wondering if Todd and I hadn't been extremely naïve to talk so openly, particularly in regard to such proprietary technology in such an early stage. Whether he intended to or not, William was doing me a favor, causing me to question the very basic assumption of privacy. Even though we were in a big, bustling city, it was true, coincidences and acquaintances were everywhere.

"Besides, what could be so private as to preclude your trusting a newsman?" he teased.

"I'm full of secrets and hidden passageways, Mr. William," I said, in my best hushed, dusky voice, trying to match the secretive tones that he'd set up for our bar-side flirtation. If that's what it was, anyway. I wasn't sure.

"I bet you are."

"I'm a scientist," I said. "An inventor."

"Ah. Beautiful *and* brilliant," he said.

"Have you ever tried it?"

"Inventing? I'm afraid I haven't," he said. "I wouldn't even know where to begin."

"That's too bad," I said.

"Enlighten a curious newsman?"

"I like to start with what I call negative thinking," I began.

"That seems counterintuitive."

"Hear me out," I said. "It just means trying to think about what any given moment is *missing*. Us, sitting here right now, drinking our beers, what do we need to make our life just a tiny bit more comfortable?"

He nodded.

"You know how people always talk about things being *almost* perfect, but if they could just have one little tweak, it would be *even better*? Whatever those gaps are, those are the inspiration for invention."

"Ah. I see what you mean."

"People who see everything like it's already a perfect, puffy pink cloud will never be able to invent anything. You've got to be able to see what's missing. Hence, negative thinking," I said.

"I'm no scientist," he said, "Much less, an inventor. I trade in facts. But I see some similarities in writing."

"Oh?" I smiled, easing into my posture a little more. We were finding common ground, the conversation, taking its own turns. I'd never experienced this with anyone before, much less, a nosy stranger I'd met in a bar.

"Yeah. A lot of stories and books come about because of painful, life-altering experiences. Or totally joyful ones," he said. "I think most people write when they are either quite sad or really happy. That's when inspiration creeps in, when they've got something they just *have* to say." He leaned closer, and the scent of his cologne collided with that of his Guinness. "It seems to me like you have something you really want to say."

I couldn't risk opening myself up any more at this point. More accurately, I didn't *want* to. Tonight was supposed to be my night off, and I'd just gotten myself all worked up thinking about all the missing pieces that Spells could correct if all went well. My thoughts began a dance in a thousand directions, and it was all I could do to stop myself from starting "to do" lists and brainstorming questions on bar napkins.

"You're right," I admitted, leaning back to make a little more space between us, the ever-shy girl that I am, squaring my body off toward the bar, rather than toward him. "But I don't want to talk about that tonight. Tonight I want to talk about anything else. The weather, even. What do you think of it?"

"I love this season," he said.

"I don't know," I said. "I could do without the heat. But it's nice after the rain, when everything seems wiped clean. Even the air on the beach is a little more breathable."

"I can almost smell love in the air, actually. Can you?" He teased.

I wasn't falling for it, not tonight anyway.

"Actually, I smell apple pie. With cinnamon," I said.

He sniffed, holding up a finger as if to signal a brilliant idea.

"You know, I think we can purchase some of that," he said, opening a small menu and pointing at it. "Yes, yes, we can."

"Can you grab a waiter and ask him to bring us over a piece? I'm going to find a table where we can continue this conversation. It's getting a little too crowded here at the bar," I said, and watched him smile from ear to ear as he surveyed the empty landscape of the barstools. We were the only ones at the bar, but I wanted to settle in and get comfortable for a while. I needed the company.

I waited for him at a booth in the back of the room, where it was quieter, away from the speakers blaring music and the crowds that had started to gather at the front of the pub. Everyone was showing up for dinner. As he approached, I admired his tall physique; I have a weakness for tall men.

He slid into the booth and asked me, "Are you in a hurry to get home . . . to anyone?"

I chuckled. "Nope. I've got no one to answer to. Not even a cat. Had a cockatiel for eighteen years, but he flew away, unfortunately. And I work my own hours, being an independent inventor and all."

"That's what I like to hear," he said. "I keep pretty late hours, since I work only in front of a computer, and usually at home."

"Why the late hours?"

"I just like to write at night. There's something about the quietness of the night. I feel like the night watchman, making sure everything is safe outside on the street where I live," he said. "In fact, there haven't been any robberies on my street since I came to live there eight years ago. My light's always on. I like to think I scare 'em off."

"So, a watchful night owl. And you sleep during the day?"

"Usually in the wee hours. I wake up around afternoon for lunch."

"And what does my mysterious night-owl friend write about?"

"I'm a technology freak, actually. So I appreciate the spirit of negative thinking that leads to inventiveness," he said. "My column is called 'The Buzz,' and it's all about the new gadgets that everyone is blogging about. I wrote a web-crawler code that crawls technology blogs and highlights what the latest buzz is about."

"So you publish what people talk about?" I asked. "No wonder you're such a good eavesdropper."

"Like you, I like to think I'm doing a public service," he said. "A conventional news reporter seeks out new technologies and somehow makes his own decision about what's in and what's out, which seems unfair to me. Arbitrary. The news I report comes from the masses themselves, according to what they blog about," he continued, making an expansive gesture to the bar, raising his glass to everyone who was looking in his way. Funny guy.

"That's fascinating," I admitted. "I wish it were a little more helpful to me, though. Nobody blogs about what I'm up to!"

"Sorry ma'am, no can do," he said. "I only do consumer tech. Not really much for biotech."

I felt myself looking a little crestfallen. It surprised me how disappointed I was that this wasn't going to be the big break. Not for me, but for Spells.

"Why the long face?" he asked.

"Ugh, just a potential investor I met," I admitted. "He made a snide remark about my technology. Said it was low-tech, not high-tech."

He shrugged. "He's a jerk. Just skip him. On to the next."

"I think I take potential investors' comments a little too seriously," I said, looking down at the scratchy booth.

Luckily for the mood, the fresh slice of apple pie arrived at the table just then, its warm cinnamon smell wafting up to our noses. The waiter had brought two forks. I noticed how polite William was to the waiter. *I should probably get out of the lab more often, no, DEFINITELY,* I thought, taking a heaping bite of the pie.

"I don't blame you," he said kindly, dividing up the melting vanilla ice cream on top so that we'd get equal shots at it. "It's hard not to take criticism too harshly, especially if you work largely alone, like we do. When the nagging voice is the loudest in the room, there's a good chance it's also the *only* voice in the room."

"Depends on how much you talk to yourself," I said, and feeling my good humor return, I gave him a sly smile. "I read that people who talk to themselves are masterminds."

We talked a little more, but then finished the pie in an amicable silence. It was getting late, and I was looking forward to sleeping in tomorrow. We said good-bye, not even exchanging our last names. Somehow, I felt it wouldn't be hard to find him again.

chapter 8

Todd had his mind set on finding us an investment as soon as possible to free us of our monetary concerns related to our research. His research on local biotech players was fruitful; we had a meeting set with Lilian Gerit, a high-powered exec with some great connections in the field.

I'd been thankful for Todd from the moment that he'd signed on, but watching him stride, confident and handsome, into the conference room to greet Gerit and her associates, I said a little thank-you to the universe that I'd found such a consummately professional partner.

"It's wonderful to meet you," he said, flashing her a warm smile. Whatever tension had hung in the clean-lined corporate air was starting to dissipate.

"Thank you for taking the time to talk with us about our proposal," I added, taking my seat beside Todd, my mouth as dry as the desert. I plucked a bottle of water from the neat pyramid sitting in the center of the table, looking at the various professionals as they thumbed through copies of our work. Gerit didn't move to introduce them; they would remain anonymous and incidental, and she clearly ran the show.

Todd opened up with our introductions, and I gave a brief overview of the application as well as the need for *in ovo* differentiation of chicks.

On Todd's advice, I kept it short and sweet, the bird's-eye view. I was also hesitant to get too far into the biological nitty-gritty; I didn't know much about business, but I knew enough that protecting my intellectual property was going to be important.

Gerit nodded, appraising what we'd brought.

"I'm impressed," she said, adding that, if successful, she wouldn't be surprised if our start-up valuation ran from $5 to $15 million. "You stand to gain quite a bit, even if you're acquired outright by an existing company."

Her well-manicured fingers twirled an expensive-looking pen.

"Tell me, have you secured a patent?"

Truthfully, these were beyond the scope of questions I was prepared to answer. I was out of my element, and I felt the room begin to close in on me a little bit. Had I made a mistake in venturing into shark-infested waters? I was a bench scientist, not a power broker. I wasn't ready to hand off the idea to a big company and lose control of the project. I wanted to be in on the excitement from the ground up.

Still, I could see that Gerit's interest was piqued. She had quickly arranged a meeting with another biotech start-up she had worked with recently whose work had just been acquired by one of those big players in the game.

"If they like your idea," she hinted, "you might not have to worry about incubating. You might just have to worry about where you're going to put your payout."

The meeting she arranged was nothing short of a disaster; it became clear to me very quickly that when Gerit intuited we didn't have a patent, she was trying to set our ideas up to be poached. They wanted to see results, gels, detailed information—the works—all without any indication that they'd be willing to sign any kind of documentation to protect our proprietary work.

I don't know where I got the strength to resist the pressure, the pull of easy money, but I continued to hold my cards close to my chest, even when I was being berated by executives as they were kicking me out the door. One of them even suggested sitting with me to explain how to present biological results, as if that was my issue.

Needless to say, I was furious. Still feeling the flush in my cheeks as I rode down in the elevator with Todd, I was getting a taste of what lay ahead; what had seemed such a simple, elegant solution to the barbaric practice of the poultry industry was not so pure to the other players. Business was business, and where there was money to be made, there were also people to walk all over on the way to the payday.

"Why would those people think I was going to share our secrets with them?"

"I'm just as confused as you are," Todd said, shaking his head. "They were unreasonable, and rude to boot."

I could sense that he was uncomfortable, like there was a small rock in the shoe of his psyche. He opened his mouth to speak, then thought the better of it.

"Do you think we did the right thing?"

He stopped walking, exhaled, and took a good look at me. For all his business acumen, the thing I valued most about Todd was his honesty. I knew he wouldn't mince words with me.

"I don't know, Scarlet," he admitted. "It would have been pretty easy money to sell our ideas to them."

I bit back my anger; Todd was just looking out for our financial interests. He wasn't like me, glued to the bench, studying the solution on the most detailed level. He was just helping with what I'd asked him to. Steadying myself, as if to remind myself that he was my friend and true ally, I put my hand on his shoulder.

"Todd, there are no freebies in life. I'm willing to work hard, and I think you are too."

He nodded, and that was the end of that conversation and the beginning of a more perfect partnership.

chapter 9

B ut that first set of meetings hadn't been a complete waste of our time. Now we understood what to prepare for, what would be expected of us when we walked into some of these boardrooms. Gerit may have been trying to take advantage of us, but she also tipped her hand; we knew now that we would need to apply for a patent. Once we had that patent, we could feel more secure about opening up to potential partners in discussions without fearing that they were trying to steal our precious secrets. I wasn't thinking of the money first and foremost; I wanted to solve the problem that was inherent to the manual method of chick sexing and destruction. But I knew deep down that these secrets were worth a good deal of money; and beyond that, I was young, and idealistic. But I am proud to say, I was not foolish.

There is a famous story about a great Russian mathematician who was once asked to be the arbiter of a quarrel between two students. One student claimed he had solved a problem that his friend had stolen and published. The professor advising the two students asked this great mathematician to intervene. The professor asked that the mathematician listen to the two students and decide who, in his opinion, was the one who had really done the work. That student would receive the final credit.

The mathematician met with the two students and listened to each make his argument. Finally, he chose the student who had published, rather than the other, and this student was given the credit. The professor of the two students later came into his office and asked the mathematician if he did not think it was the second student who'd really done the work. "Personally," the professor added, "I think it was the second student."

The mathematician replied quickly, "Of course I know he did the work. But that second young man will have many good ideas in his career. He doesn't need this particular credit to prove his intelligence. The student who stole? It might be his only chance for success. We might as well let him have it."

When you get that first idea, an idea that you believe to be great, you hold on to it tightly. In fact, you sometimes hold on so tightly that people start to begrudge you for it. This was how I felt about the sexing application. On the one hand, I wanted everyone to leave me alone, to let me work on my project, solve the problem, and get on with the science. But on the other hand, I didn't want to alienate potential investors. I needed money to make this project a reality, so I needed them to think that something big was cooking behind the scenes. It was a delicate balance.

Todd, on the other hand, wasn't as paralyzed by this kind of indecision. He set up meeting after meeting until we would secure an investment. With Lauralynn's kindness and assistance, we reached out to every one of her contacts whom she shared with us. She gave us the names and details of anyone she could think of who would possibly meet the terms of a potential investor and allowed us to use her conference space as a neutral meeting ground.

But the first thing on our list was to meet with a patent attorney with whom Lauralynn had set us up, Patrick Stockwell. She said he was the best patent attorney in the state.

"Great," I said, rolling my eyes. "Then we better find an investor soon enough to finance it, because it will probably cost us an arm and a leg."

Stockwell's office was on the fifty-first floor of a skyscraper located across from Lauralynn's building. His window faced the opposite side of the city, so we had a birds-eye view of our beloved home base. Todd and I sat, sipping coffee and quietly enjoying the view until the meeting started.

Stockwell breezed into the room without so much as an introduction, sliding into a seat at the end of the glass conference table.

"We're talking $15K," he said.

"And what exactly does that include?" Todd jumped right in.

"Initial preparation of the patent, which includes writing a summary of the idea and the claims. Then, we'll file the application at the patent office and handle the case from there. Our lawyers are highly qualified and each has a Ph.D. in the required field, plus a law degree, of course," he said.

I gulped and looked around. No wonder they could afford such luxurious digs.

"I, myself, have a Ph.D. in physics from Harvard, as it happens," said Stockwell.

A slim, blonde woman entered the room and smiled at Stockwell, looking for his cue. Once he'd nodded to her, she sat down and faced us. He must have gathered we were, indeed, serious.

"This is Donna Burton," he said. "She's our bio-patent expert, and she'll be handling your patent, should you choose to retain our services."

I opened my mouth to ask for a moment to consider, but Todd gave me the eye. I could tell he was already sold.

Donna smiled warmly and opened up a file that Stockwell had prepared.

"So, your company's name is 'Spells'? That is an interesting name," she said.

"It comes from our product," I said, "which is essentially a spell-checker for DNA. We want to identify specific sequences."

"I love the spell-checker enzymes," said Donna, and a feeling of gratitude washed over me. I had to thank Lauralynn for sending us here, no matter the price tag.

"It's nice to meet a fellow geek," I said to Donna with a smile, "and I mean that in the best way possible."

"I gladly accept the compliment," she said.

Stockwell took over to talk about procedure.

"What we usually do is write the patent in as general terms as we can, keeping in mind the scope of the idea, and then we narrow it down according to the examiner's comments. The summary includes an introductory to the patent subject and references and other related ideas or patents that may influence the judgment of the patent. It also summarizes the other known methods. The claims are then the only thing the inventor claims as his or her invention. It is the only thing that is legally binding in the patent. Anything that is not written down in the claims, is not owned by the inventor."

"Who is the inventor here?" asked Donna.

"I am," I answered.

"This is an important distinction," explained Donna. "The patent owner and inventor are two different things. The inventor usually gets credit for the invention, but ownership is given to the company, which pays the inventor's salary. That means the inventor is not the legal owner of the patent; the company is."

"Will I have to write the patent?" I asked.

"No," said Stockwell. "You'll be working with Donna on that. You'll explain your idea in detail and she'll write out the claims. It's your job to be explicit in your explanation of the idea and what exactly you claim as your own invention, so that Donna can do her job well."

"What is considered an invention?" I asked hesitantly. I had once taken for granted that I knew the answer to this question, but now that we'd stepped into the complicated world of legalese, I wasn't sure which end was up.

"An invention, in legal terms, is defined as a new, useful, and nonobvious process, machine, or product or an improvement of an existing one," Donna explained politely, waxing into more about patent law, trademarks, copyrights, intellectual property, and more. That she could be an expert in biotech and this esoteric type of law astounded me. I knew she must have been truly brilliant.

It wasn't long after that moment that we signed a retainer and agreed to work with Donna. We set up a separate meeting with her, agreeing to be in touch by e-mail and phone and have a meeting once every two weeks in order to get the patent completed as soon as possible.

chapter 10

Todd and I were meeting for business talk one night at what had quickly become our stomping ground, the Flying Cow. When he finished his beer, he stood up to go, and made a motion as if he were waiting for me to leave too. I shook my head.

"I think I'll sit for a while," I said. "You know, stay out in the world a little bit before I get back to the lab."

The truth was, I was embarrassed about my motivation. I was hoping that I'd run into the cute newsman again. Blessedly, Todd didn't make any inquiries, and soon I was left absentmindedly eating nuts and watching the muted news and sportscasts on the TVs behind the bar. After half an hour, I'd given up hope. I decided that I'd visit the restroom before walking back home.

Winding my way back through the crowd, I suddenly saw him sitting at a back booth. He had a pile of papers in front of him and was reading. As I walked closer, I saw an undisturbed slice of apple pie sitting on a plate across the table from him. Gingerly, I looked around for a jacket or some sign of a date on that side of the table, and was pleased to find no such thing.

"May I join you?" I asked. "Or does this pie belong to someone?"

"I was saving this seat for someone who likes cinnamon apple pie," he said, smiling. "That wouldn't happen to be you, by any chance, would it?"

I blushed. "Of course, good sir. I love cinnamon apple pie."

He stood up and grandly motioned to my side of the booth, taking my hand to guide me as I slid in, in front of the pie. It smelled perfectly delicious, and I was so happy I'd decided to wait. That feeling wasn't just about the pie, though, obviously.

He sat back down. "I should probably ask the waiter to warm it up for us," he said. "It's been sitting here waiting for you for a long time."

I couldn't believe that he'd been waiting for me. He must have seen me when he came in, I thought with a smile. He motioned for the waiter, who took the pie away to warm it back up. The place was crowded with people and the music was loud, so I had to strain to hear William when he spoke. But his eyes shined clear at me from across the table; he had the most amazing eyes.

"And what have you been up to?" he asked.

"A lot, actually," I said with a laugh. I couldn't contain my emotion; it felt so right to be here with him. I told him everything, practically my whole life story. I was thrilled and nervous, and he could tell. Luckily, he thought I was funny—or at the very least, amusing. He laughed along, asking me questions as my words spilled out.

At some point, I noted his questions were a little too perfect, a little too pointed.

"For someone who didn't know anything about the poultry business when we last spoke, you seem like you know a little more about what's at stake today," I said.

"I have to confess, I did some research after we last saw one another," he said.

"And? What did you find?"

"Plenty about chickens. Not much about chicken sexing, unfortunately," he said. "No one on the bioblogs is really talking about it."

"No buzz, huh?"

"Nada. I searched under 'green' and 'cleantech,' too, just to be sure," he said. "My algorithm is very good. Incidentally, you wouldn't believe what you get if you just type 'chick sexing' into Google."

I laughed. "So. You've been snooping around behind my back."

"You caught my curiosity," he said. "What can I say?"

I was silent, speechless for once. I took a bite of the pie and solicitously offered up my fork. "Any for you?"

"I wouldn't dream of stealing your pie," he said. "You seem to be enjoying it too much." He called the waiter over for another beer. "If I'm being entirely truthful, I didn't totally come up empty-handed."

"Do tell," I said, somewhat terrified that he had found an embarrassing old school photograph to gloat over.

"I did find a lead," he said, leaning over and lowering his voice. "It looks like there are some negotiations going on between the company that owns the injection-machine technology and a huge pharmaceutical company."

"RICPCom?" I was incredulous. Surely they would have mentioned this. "And who?"

He nodded. "I mean, *huge*." He made a motion with his hands to signal thumbing through a wad of cash. "I'm not sure what the deal is going to be about, but there's a lot of talk."

I was confused; I was accustomed to doing plenty of my own searching, and I hadn't found a thing.

"How did you find this out?" I asked, leaning over, my voice straining to stay quiet but still be heard over the din of the bar.

"Let's just say it's not information that's readily available to the public," he said. "Not in the public domain, as it were."

"Oh-em-gee! You're a HACKER!?" My voice rose involuntarily. I quickly regretted it.

"Shhh," he admonished.

"Sorry!" I put my hand over my mouth.

"It's OK. You just can't be too careful," he said with a wink. "You never know who's sitting in these bars snooping around."

"I can't believe you'd do this for me," I said.

"Hold your horses, cowgirl," he shot back. "I didn't say anything about doing this for you."

I don't think he meant it to, but the remark stung. *Of course,* I thought. *How could I be so foolish as to think this had anything to do with me?*

But then, in a joking tone, he added, "I did it for the fun of it."

I smiled. "Well, in any case, I'm grateful."

"I'm a newsman, after all," he said. "Knowledge is everything to me."

I decided to press my luck. "Well, if you, by any chance, happen upon any more knowledge about that sector . . ."

He winked again, reaching his hand across the table to tap mine, folded in front of my empty pie plate.

"You know, I do have a question for you about something I read," he said.

"Yes?"

"When do you plan to sex the chicks in the egg? On what day?" he asked.

"We are planning to piggyback on the day the vaccines are injected: day eighteen. Then we can draw a sample for our sexing test. But we hope to get down to the tenth day for our next-generation product," I explained.

"Is taking thousands of eggs out of incubation twice really convenient, though? Once for the sexing and once for the inoculating?" he asked.

I could see his point.

"It does take time. But where are you going with this?"

"My point is that the way these incubators are structured, it takes a lot of careful practice to get all these eggs onto the conveyor belts safely, and if you do it twice, you would be risking more trays falling and further product loss. I think you have to think this through. It may not be such a bad idea to wait until hatching day," William explained.

I wanted to control my anger, but I could feel my face turning red.

"William, are you saying I shouldn't pursue my project because the workers can't handle moving trays with caution? I think we can give them more credit than that! Plus, this is important!"

His reply was gentle, calm. "I am just pointing out that the poultry-industry people have their way of doing things and it may appear as interference on your part, trying to change things. Some things are better left untouched."

"I don't understand, William," I said. I was baffled by his comment. "I thought you would be on my side, encouraging me! You seemed like a guy who takes on challenges, not runs away from them. As a reporter who seeks the truth, I thought your moral judgments would prevail. RICPCom's injection technology changed the industry. They went from inoculating by hand to automated inoculation, reducing the manual handling of chicks and disease transfer."

"You're right," he said. "I should and will support you. And I will also continue to be on the lookout for anything my crawler finds on the poultry sector on the Net."

He stared into my eyes quietly and gently put his hand back on mine again as if to reassure me he meant no harm.

"William," I said, rubbing a nascent tear from my eye. I was embarrassed to be so emotional. "I think I have something in my eye," I claimed, leaning over to him and opening up my left eye widely. "Do you mind checking?"

Ever the gentleman, he didn't make a big deal of my waterworks. He looked into my eye intently, holding on to that moment for just a few seconds longer, my face so close to his.

"Nope, it's fine, nothing there," he said.

"Thank you," I said, sitting back in my seat. "Must have been allergies."

I melted, and thought about that moment for the rest of the evening until I finally found sleep around midnight.

chapter 11

The next potential investor on our call sheet was another heavyweight. George Roseword had sold a high-tech engineering company a few years back for millions; I had a tangential connection in my friend Paul, a software engineer who had worked for him in the summers. I had learned quickly from Todd that no matter how fragile a connection might seem, you need to work it for all it is worth. So I reached out. I was surprised when I received an e-mail from Roseword's partner, Samuel Cole, who said they'd be interested in talking things out.

Paul had prepared me for a lengthy process; first, Cole would vet the idea, and then, if he liked it, he'd send it up the chain to see if Roseword wanted to meet. I had prepared Paul to assist in the meeting by explaining the idea of Spells to him. I was nervous, but convinced myself that trusting Paul was worth the risk.

We made our way to Cole's office, which was located at Sea and Sun, a live/work complex overlooking the sea. As soon as Cole welcomed us in, I took in the terrace with an amazing view. I hoped he'd invite us out onto the terrace, but instead, we clustered around the living room table, and Paul booted up a laptop.

To my surprise, Cole started the meeting not by asking questions about Spells, but rather, discussing a subject that interested him.

He wanted to translate our spell-checker method so that it could be retrofitted into a chip—the smaller, the better of course.

"But biochip technology already exists," I said, "as I'm sure you're aware."

Cole waved me off dismissively. "Yes, I know," he said. "But we can make it better, not to mention, smaller. With our experience in electrical engineering and your experience with the bio side of the house, I'm sure we can think of a more efficient way to get this done."

Cole sounded confident, but to be honest, *I* wasn't so confident. I was already feeling a pressure that was bound to break the fragile bridge of my inspiration, my process. This wasn't how I was used to working; instead, I found problems I was interested in and solved them in my own way, on my own time, intuitively, because I felt inspired. If I wanted to solve something, it was because I felt I had the tools to do it. Meanwhile, Cole was asking me to come up with ideas and solutions on commission.

It wasn't that I wasn't familiar with the subject; in fact, I'd read a lot about biochips even before I'd started working on the chicken project. Single genetic alterations in DNA are important for detecting differences in genetic information, which may cause differences in normal characteristics or may alter genes to form disease. Cole wanted to use our technology on a biochip to detect these single nucleotide polymorphisms (SNPs), whereas I wanted to test them with my assay. I wasn't at all sure if his way was better, and furthermore, I had to hide my own solution to the same problem because I'd learned that until we had our patents in order, our intellectual property was low-hanging fruit for anyone savvy enough to snatch it from us. Still, I wanted to get on Cole's good side in hopes of eventually meeting with Roseword and securing an investment; thus, on I pressed with the hypotheticals.

Suddenly, as if I'd conjured him, Roseword appeared at the door. Short, stocky, and sporting an amazing tan, with eyes like sharpened points of granite that looked like they could cut you open, he clearly meant business. He had the look of an Air Force fighter pilot. Cole was caught off guard. He introduced Roseword, and immediately sat down to make way for Roseword at what was essentially the head of the table.

While I'd felt that things were getting away from me earlier in the meeting, now they were on a high-speed train in the wrong direction. I saw we would no longer be talking about Spells, but rather, about the biochip that Cole was obsessing over. Paul nodded emphatically, taking notes on his laptop, and I began to question to whom his loyalty really belonged. At the same time, it felt like there was nothing for me to lose; this wasn't my idea, and I wasn't going to be left exposed to Roseword and Cole's opinion of that idea.

Roseword had his share of questions; it seemed like he was well-read on the matter. But the train came to a screeching halt when he began to direct his questions to Paul, and Paul alone. It became clear that Roseword thought Paul and I were business partners, rather than understanding that Paul was just brought on to consult.

"So you two are in business together?" he asked.

Before I could answer, Paul had taken over and was holding court.

"Yes," said Paul. "Scarlet is working on something else," he began while I started to grind my teeth in horror, realizing he was talking about Spells, "but it might not pan out. In the meantime, she and I can go forward with this idea."

He'd shot me down.

I couldn't help it; something halfway between a gasp and a laugh came out of my mouth.

"I'm sorry?" I said, looking at Paul. I know that if Todd had been there, he could have walked me back from the brink, but as it stood, I was all alone and there was no turning back. "I wasn't aware of this plan, Paul. I strongly believe in what I'm working on now, and I have every intention of following through. In no way did I say I would close my company or forgo my plans."

"I'm sorry," Paul stammered. "I just assumed—"

Cole turned red, embarrassed for having wasted his counterpart's time. It was clear who really ran the operation. Roseword coolly assessed us both with glinting, vulpine eyes before speaking.

"I think we're done here for now," he said, getting up and motioning toward the door.

It was unfortunate that Paul and I had shared a ride there. Worse than arguing all the way home, we didn't speak to one another.

Two days later, I was taking a break from the bench when I checked my e-mail. There was a message there from Roseword. He said he was impressed with the presentation, despite the hiccups, and wanted to hear more. But first, he said, he wanted to ask me some questions about a project of his. Wanting to build bridges that I had feared I'd burned in my disagreement with Paul, I agreed, and we e-mailed back and forth for a good while. Nights, days, weekends, holidays, all these didn't matter to him, and I liked that about him. I felt we shared the same energy and were on the same page workwise. I was familiar with his questions and he was grateful for my advice. Every time I saw an e-mail from him, whether it was at two o'clock in the morning or on a holiday, I jumped at the chance to answer and show off my expertise. Although I was still a bit miffed that he had been more interested in Paul's thoughts than mine, and in Cole's idea rather than my own technology for Spells, I tried to remember that you catch more flies with honey than with vinegar, and I worked my hardest to be the resource he needed.

At the end of the exchange, there it was: the golden key.

"I'd love to hear more about your passion project," he said. "I think we should meet and talk about your company."

After I had convinced Roseword that I knew enough about others' ideas, he was willing to give me an hour to express mine. I was ecstatic, and called Todd immediately, exhilarated.

"Roseword wants to meet with us. This might be our big chance."

We arranged the meeting for one night the following week at Roseword's home. I had suggested a café or even Lauralynn's office, but Roseword was having none of it. I tried to picture the clean-lined designer pieces all arranged just so in his living room, tried to think about how such a power player would adorn his nest. I was intimidated, but not enough to be scared off. Why not see how the other half lives, I thought. It's not every day you get invited into the lion's den.

Needless to say, I immediately went out and bought a new suit. I had prepared a speech and gone over it with Todd while he was practicing his marketing skills on me. I didn't prepare any lab results, but rather, worked on crafting an analogy that was simple enough to understand and to capture the attention of these engineers. Regardless of how beautiful the science was, I kept telling myself that I needed to make it accessible, understandable, and—above all—irresistible.

The suit won't hurt either, I thought. *It's a nice change from my daily lab coat.* I smiled as I slid it back onto the hanger, where it would wait its turn until the main event.

chapter 12

After the debacle with Paul, I didn't want to bring in anyone else to infect or change the ideas that were at the heart of Spells. Todd, ever the pragmatist, convinced me otherwise. He said that in order for us to have the strongest position possible, we needed an inside link to Roseword and Cole.

"Even though we had already met with them?"

"Uh-huh."

I sighed, feeling myself capitulating against my better judgment. Todd was the business mind, after all. I racked my brain and my virtual rolodex to see whom I might know who might be able to help us out in this department, and came up with my friend Joel Drafford, a young, friendly entrepreneur who had just begun his own start-up journey. Before that, he had worked with Roseword and Cole on a previous venture.

He said he'd be happy to talk to me in advance of my meeting with Roseword, and we soon convened for lunch at the university where we both studied. I had a meeting earlier that day with an old professor, and he often went there to avail himself of the research resources. We bagged our lunches like in the old days and secreted away to my old corner by the philosophy building.

"Scarlet! It's been too long," he said, opening up his lunch bag and peering inside, as if he would be surprised by the contents. "This is so exciting that you're meeting with George Roseword to talk about potential business ideas."

My smile came naturally; this wasn't just any ordinary networking meeting I had to push through. I was genuinely happy to see an old friend.

"Yes," I said. "He's an impressive man. I imagine he was a great boss, too."

Joel nodded, cocking his head as if remembering the good old days.

"I do miss that security sometimes," he said. "You know, the regular paycheck, the other people backing you."

"How's your big project going these days?" I asked, hoping I wasn't being too intrusive.

"It's good, but it's going slowly," he said, lowering his voice and looking to make sure we were truly alone. "We're developing equipment that will detect small quantities of viral or bacterial DNA to sniff out bio-warfare threats, like detecting anthrax on an envelope."

"That's exactly what I need!" I exclaimed.

He laughed. "Are you in that much trouble?"

"No," I said, shaking my head. "I'm under no threat. I just need it for some chickens I'm working with."

"This is just getting stranger and stranger," he said.

"It's not what it sounds like," I shot back.

"Scarlet," he said, a friendly hand on my arm, "I'm not even sure what it sounds like!"

"I need a way to assess DNA in microscopic amounts, because it's almost nonexistent in the blood I draw from blood vessels inside of the egg shells of the chickens I'm working on. I've been looking for alternatives to amplify the signal from that DNA, as it were," I said.

I almost choked on my sandwich when he clapped me on the back.

"My dear! You have come to the right place!" he exclaimed.

"What do you mean?"

"There's no need to amplify. We've got a super-cool technique to enhance the signal-to-noise ratio right here," he said.

"Don't play with my heart, Joel," I said.

"Would I do that to you?"

I had to admit, I didn't think so. Joel wasn't like the villainous, cutthroat entrepreneurs that one sees in Hollywood films. He was all heart, a truly decent man. Furthermore, he was a community man; he taught kids basketball and joined the city's Parent Patrol, a group of parents who volunteer within their community, spending their free time on the streets, making sure their presence is felt at the youth hangout spots.

They communicate with the teens and explain the dangers of drug and alcohol abuse.

The Patrol acts in cooperation with law-enforcement officials, helping to prevent crime in the community.

"When can I come over to see your setup?" I asked, half joking but hoping he'd take me seriously.

"Come over tomorrow," he replied without hesitation, standing up and brushing the crumbs off his khakis. "Your application sounds intriguing, and besides, we've only been working with synthetic DNA. Maybe if you scratch my back, I'll scratch yours," he said with a wink.

We began to walk together out into the courtyard, and the possibilities warmed me as much as did the sun's heat.

"I'm so glad you might be able to help out, Joel," I said, explaining that the superior design had a hand in chicken blood, which would also help us out in the amplification department. DNA was present in Chicken's red *and* white blood cells, as opposed to in human samples, where it is only present in the white ones. This means we would have more DNA per each sample of blood. I took it as a sign that chickens were *meant* to be sexed in the egg; if they did not have this characteristic, it would be an impossible task to undertake.

"Life works in mysterious ways," I said.

"Ain't that the truth," he agreed, giving me a final smile and a wave as he went off to pursue his own work.

The next day, I met with Joel at his lab, and got a chance to see his equipment. The idea behind all the shiny high technology was simple, but his device was elegant, and it took a team of ten, working together in a large, loft-like space, to execute his engineering concept.

"Joel," I said, surveying the space. "You should be proud."

He beamed. "That means a lot, coming from you, Scarlet."

chapter 13

The time had come for our meeting at Roseword's home, a hulking Brutalist house set on top of a high hill. It felt ten degrees cooler on the hilltop, even in the summer heat. Roseword took us into the house and we saw, but were not introduced to, a teenaged boy playing a game of virtual tennis on a huge TV screen. He was moving from side to side of the living room, his hand making sweeping motions that coincided with the *THOCK* of the virtual ball through the surround-sound system. Outdoor tennis seemed to be moving toward obsolescence.

As we started making our way down the hall to Roseword's office, he had a change of heart and guided us outside onto the deck, where he joined Cole at a long table overlooking the craggy mountainous vistas behind the house. I was hoping for something a little more intimate, or at least, something a little warmer. The sun was setting, it was growing cooler by the moment, and it seemed as though he had no inclination to turn on the lights. Only Roseword seemed unaffected by the temperature.

I took a deep breath, and then began my speech, detailing how their idea of biochips was a hot topic at the moment, especially since there was a push to read a person's entire genetic information—or Genome—for $1,000.

"Currently, it can be done for $10,000; not exactly pocket change," I said, and they nodded in stony silence. "If we could each get our genetic data on a CD, we would potentially know, someday, which types of diseases we are prone to and we could receive personalized treatment for our specific problems. No more general drugs that target general receptors in our bodies; instead, we will use a drug that inhibits the exact source of our illness."

I could tell I had their attention; I was on a roll. Now would be the time to persuade them away from the chip technology they had alluded to in my first disastrous meeting with Paul and onto my assay idea.

"The DNA is the genetic information, which is transferred from generation to generation, and each species has its unique genome. If you can imagine a book that is copied over and over, you can also imagine that while the book is copied, spelling errors may occur," I said, incorporating the "spell-checker" that was at the heart of Spells.

"Rather than having you read this book line by line checking for errors, our assay technology works as a 'spell-checker,' inferring by subtraction," I explained.

"As we said in the first meeting," Cole began, "we're interested in chip-based solutions."

I felt put down again, and unsure why Cole was so adamant about chip-based solutions.

"I understand that, but given the size of our operation, your goal is a little out of our reach. There are huge companies with hundreds of employees trying to work on this problem, and we feel that we want to take on something that we can handle. I absolutely would love the chance to work with you, and that's why I'm willing to consider talking out these solutions with you. But I have to admit, I would appreciate the opportunity to explain the real reason why we are here."

Then, I felt a sharp kick under the table. Todd didn't look too amused by my choice of words. I tried to finesse things a little bit.

"What I meant to say is that I'd love the opportunity, if you'll allow it, to explain an application I'm very passionate about."

Cole appeared restless, while Roseword seemed interested. He leaned into the table a bit, motioning for me to continue.

"This does sound interesting," he said, while I could detect Cole trying to keep his eyes from rolling.

Seeing the opening, I jumped right in.

"Chickens," I said, grinning from ear to ear. That caught their attention, if only by seeming to be a non sequitur. *Had they really invited a madwoman out to their ten-million-dollar property to waste their time?* they surely wondered.

Todd sensed that I was getting overexcited and tried to turn the pitch to one that operated on a level businesspeople understood: money.

"The poultry industry trashes two billion male chicks each year, worldwide," he said. "They might as well be burning their money with that loss. We'd like to turn this loss into profit."

Now, even Cole was listening. Todd continued.

"As you know, the world is going green, and so must we. If we can determine if these chicks are male while still in the egg, the egg white can be used for different products made from egg-white powder. We would save on incubation time and electricity. All this translates into profits."

"What does this have to do with genetic information and chips?" asked Cole. "I would like to stay on the subject at hand. Honestly, John—"

Here, with a swift motion of his hand, Roseword cut him off.

"It has *everything* to do with this," I explained. "If you take the genetic information of a female chicken, it differs from the male information. This is similar to the comparison of human genetic information, but here, we are comparing chicken genetic information in order to ascertain the sex of the chick."

"So you picked one application, and you are going to show that your method works?" asked Roseword.

"Yes," I said. "My simple example shows that I can differentiate between female and male chickens by subtracting their genetic differences." I paused, waiting to see their reaction.

"And so you've essentially found a way to test your method on a small scale," Roseword said. "I love it!"

"I love it, too," I said, smiling first at Todd, and then beaming at Cole, who was forced to stay quiet while Todd went on with the marketing end of the presentation.

I finally relaxed, sipping from a glass of water and glancing inside to see how the tennis game was going in the living room. My mind was wandering off to happy places, where I could work in a lab without having to worry about money.

"I like your story, Scarlet," said Roseword. "I came here expecting to talk about DNA on chips, which everyone seems to be talking about. But your explanation of why that technology is important came with an exciting twist. You managed to show me that you think within your reach, and I rarely see that in young entrepreneurs. They all seem to bite off more than they can chew." He motioned to Todd. "And plus, your partner here has convinced me that there is money to be made."

"It's a bit low-tech, John," Cole sneered. "Do you think it's enough profit for our investment firm to consider?"

Roseword did not hesitate. "I don't care about the firm. I'm putting $100K down on Spells out of my own pocket."

It takes a conscientious man to rise to the occasion.

I nearly fainted, but Todd managed to pull me out of there before I made a complete fool out of myself, profusely thanking Roseword and even Cole, who had nothing to do with it. Unfortunately, as it turned out, I was not good at keeping my cool.

"We found our Angel," I said to Todd on our way out, meaning our angel investor—a successful businessman willing to invest some of his own capital on our big dreams. And now Spells was four: Todd, Joel—our temporary partner, Roseword, and I. I couldn't wait to have Roseword officially on board, even though I knew he'd want a board position with a consulting role and a veto vote. I was nervous about giving up some of my control, but the money soothed that blow. And besides, he was an engineer; maybe he wouldn't want to see anything more detailed than a quarterly report, I rationalized.

If I'd learned one thing from the business books Todd had loaned me over the course of our time together, it was that you should spend a lot of time getting to know angel investors, because you're going to be spending a lot of time with them in the future—a crucial time in your business life. That was easier said than done for us; we were under time constraints, as are most people in the start-up line of work. One doesn't find an angel every day. Isn't that why they are called angels? Normally, they're high up there in Heaven, and if they come down to visit, it's not very often that you can just take your time to get to know them before you say yes.

I thought of Charlotte in one of my favorite books, *Pride and Prejudice*. Although she was speaking about marriage, I thought the sentiment also applied to relationships with angel investors:

• •

Happiness in marriage is entirely a matter of chance. If the dispositions of the parties are ever so well known to each other or ever so similar beforehand, it does not advance their felicity in the least. They always continue to grow sufficiently unlike afterwards to have their share of vexation; and it is better to know as little as possible of the defects of the person with whom you are to pass your life.

• •

This is why, when Roseword offered to invest, I said yes right away.

And for a change, my instincts were right on the money; Roseword was nothing less than Mr. Right. He wanted a 10 percent stake in the company, which was fair and would help protect his investment. We agreed not to take certain actions without consulting him first, but, to my relief, he did not demand a veto vote. Instead, we were only to consult with him on selling the company's assets, issuing additional stock and antidilution provisions, which meant that if the business issued stock at a lower price than what he paid, he would receive additional stock. Other than that, he only asked that Todd and I would be in touch once we reached the milestones we had agreed upon, and that we would notify him of any perceivable difficulties we might encounter.

He was more than an angel come down from Heaven; for the time being, he was also our dream come true.

chapter 14

Now that money wasn't a pressing concern, I felt the world expanding in front of me. I could now sign a lease with Splice Incubators for the next year, using all of the equipment in the building to run my experiments. I could afford to buy more sophisticated materials and kits that would help enhance and expedite results.

Still, I was quite frugal, and I appreciated everything I bought. I had developed the habit of being so frugal that sometimes I would save old materials that should be trashed, but I held on to them just in case I could use them once more. Every time I purchased a new kit, I felt like a child getting a new toy, thrumming with excitement as if assembling a puzzle, from the opening of the bag and taking out all the pieces to the moment when that last piece clicks in and the picture appears.

Today's molecular biology is mostly done with kits, which means you buy the ingredients ready-made and follow the protocol: easy as ABC. The tubes are usually color-coded, and the stickers used for labeling are fun and colorful. It recalled for me that first day of school, when I'd open up my pencil case and arrange my fresh, new school supplies.

The science of it all is still difficult, but the logistics are not as difficult as they used to be. At one time, scientists would pipette by mouth, and had to weigh and calculate everything, spending precious time calibrating systems that are now on autopilot. That is not to say that everything is already determined. Research still needs standardizing, of course, but the general practice has become easier, which leaves more time and room for carefully setting up the question of the experiment. Still, if one maintains one's own lab, 90 percent of the work is maintenance—buying materials, daily setup and prep, getting rid of waste, etc.—and 10 percent is the fun part: running experiments.

It takes time to acquire independence in a lab and since there are always new things developing and new protocols, it's difficult to keep up that independence without asking others. In a shared lab space, this is where your lab mates come in, even if you're not working on the same project or even, as was the case in the incubator, for the same company. Sometimes it's more like cooking; if you just read the recipe from a cookbook without asking a seasoned chef, you might miss out on the secret tip of adding nutmeg to your carrot soup to give it that extra *oomph!*

Still, even with all of that overhead, it's still so addictive, and the sense of accomplishment simply can't be described. When I got that initial investment, I jumped right in, feeling like I could dance and sing my way through my first day back in the lab.

And, in fact, I was so grateful to Roseword, that that's exactly what I did.

Later that evening, I felt as though I could sing and dance all the way to the pub to meet William. The feeling was so infectious, I just had to do it. As he saw me coming toward him with a shy smile, he returned my smile and then some, his eyes shining. It was a sight I will never forget. I decided then and there that this time, we were going to get to know each other better. Besides, talking to hackers had always been a secret pleasure of mine.

"What's with the smile?" he asked, almost laughing.

"A lot, actually," I said with a laugh. "I got an investment. A hundred thou, no less! I'm not quite sure how we did it so fast, but we did."

"We?" he asked, his eyebrows giving a conspiratorial wiggle.

I thought about that time I had looked around his table for evidence of a date, and wondered if he was doing the same thing now, trying to sort out if I was available, if I was interested. Yes and yes. He must have felt me wondering about his motives for the question, because he waved it off as quickly as it had slipped out.

"Well, congratulations. I am happy for you," he said, raising his glass in a toast.

I laughed and clinked an imaginary glass to his.

"I noticed you don't eat much. Can I invite you to dinner with me to celebrate?" I asked, thinking that a way to a man's heart is through his stomach.

"Thanks, I eat dinner later, since I wake up late. I usually eat just fruit for lunch. But we can certainly order anything you like," he said.

"Just fruit? Wow! And what did you have for breakfast, if I may ask?"

"Just coffee," he said. "I don't eat much."

"I am so jealous," I smiled. "I have a sweet tooth, but I also love pickles."

"You should try pickle chocolate sometime."

I laughed at the absurdity of it, and blushed at his attention.

"How do you like your coffee?"

"Hot."

"Yeah," I smiled. "Cream and sugar? I just want to know in case I need to make you some. You know, sometime."

"Yes, cream and sugar, please."

"OK, great."

I smiled at him, and our eyes lingered on each other's for a moment. I tried to shake off my feelings and get myself together.

After clearing my throat, I said, "So, I was in the lab today and got new kits for my experiments. I am so excited to have the resources. I love those biology kits and I follow the instructions to the letter."

"You do?" he asked, genuinely interested.

"Yes, my father taught me early on in life how to read and follow instruction manuals. People go to so much trouble to write them and make them simple. The least we can do is follow them carefully! I can also follow instructions to fix electricity and pipes in my home."

"Quite the power-girl you are, huh? Get your toolbox ready and teach me a few things. I am pretty handy, myself."

"Glad to hear it," I said. "My dad taught me to read instructions even though he can't fix anything if his life depended on it. He has two left hands, as they say, but a good heart."

"So you fix things better than he does?"

"Yes, I have my mother's hands and a good sense of abstract thinking. You can count on me." Hesitantly, I added, "I only wish love came with a manual."

"You don't need to read up on love. It comes naturally."

"Yes, but if it only came with directions of how to make your partner happy, I could do it much more easily. And women—men can never figure them out; if they only came with instructions!" I said, clearly joking.

"You are right about that one point, but if a woman loves a man, she will open up to him and trust him."

"I will write down a manual to my heart and e-mail it to you, so you can read it. And when we meet next, I shall test you on it."

"I will be happy to study it closely and after that, I will take an exam on it, but I must warn you, I rarely fail," he remarked with a devilish smile. "I even prefer the practical exam."

"Hashtag naughty. Do you like to study on a table or the couch?"

"I start from the table, then move to the couch, then end up in bed. What about you?" he said, our earlier flirtation burning off but not the blush in my cheeks.

"I am a couch-studier; when I sit at the table, it's usually on the bench for work."

"Did you study alone or with your mom or dad, as a kid?"

"My dad was always with me to help me work out what I couldn't understand."

"Yes, mine too. Every child should have parents like that. I am very proud of my upbringing."

"Yes, so am I. Our parents gave us good values."

"Do you have a close-knit family?"

"Yes, we were very close when I grew up," he offered. "But since I moved out of town, I mainly see them on holidays now and again. I talk to my mother quite often because she is always worried about me. You?"

"My parents and my brother and I are very close," I said, feeling myself open up more. "I love to sit and have long talks with my dad. He reads a lot and always finds something to laugh about with me. I can ask him anything and he always knows the answer. It is very reassuring," I said. "When I was a kid, the thing I loved most was that he would read to us at bedtime. I still love being read to before falling asleep."

"Then I guess you found the right man for the job, me being a writer. I also love to read and I would be happy to read to you sometime," he said in his husky voice.

Soon after, we parted ways at the pub and said good night, and I was left to imagine what his reading voice might be like.

chapter **15**

S oon, the whole team was meeting with Roseword again at his house to discuss the collaboration. It was beginning to feel real, and unlike the last meeting we'd had, Cole wasn't there to muck things up. I was much more relaxed; we all knew each other and there was no question that we were all on the same team.

"I hear from Scarlet that you've got your machine up and running, Joel," Roseword began, "and that you're testing it on synthetic DNA."

"Righto," said Joel before Todd gave him a look to indicate that he needed to back off his informal tone a little bit. "Er, um, *yes*. That's correct."

"As you know, we're trying to examine DNA from the egg, which we believe is a better option than the one considered by our competitors," I said. "They're trying to determine the sex by hormone levels."

"Why is that?" Roseword asked.

"Testing the hormones in a sample taken from the egg turns out to be correct only 85 percent of the time, which leaves the margins for error wide open," I said. "DNA should provide a more precise result because genetics never lie."

Roseword nodded; again, I was so thankful to Todd, who taught me that it all had to come back to the bottom line. But I wanted to be forthright.

"Although, our method, too, has its drawbacks. First, there will be an undeniable small percentage of chicks that have a genetic disorder, which results in an abnormal number of sex chromosomes. This should produce a 2 to 3 percent error rate."

"That's manageable," said Roseword, considering the options. "And how does Joel's technology fit in, exactly?"

I was happy to explain and let Roseword in on some of Joel's brilliant work.

"The samples we take might have DNA that exists in low quantities, prohibiting our ability to detect it. We want to be ready if this indeed becomes a problem, and that's why we initiated the collaboration with Joel. He has developed a machine that has high sensing capability. Our biology, along with his engineering, is a winning strategy!"

The science was solid, and now it was Todd's turn to talk about the financial aspects of the collaboration. Once we had combined our technologies to form a machine that simultaneously draws samples out of eggs and lays them on a detection plate, we could sell the machine for $200,000 to $300,000, as well as the biological reactions per each segregated egg.

"The pricing structure is very similar to how they handle inoculations *in ovo*," said Todd. "This means you get paid for every egg you separate. That adds up to a lot of eggs."

"I love it," said Roseword, speaking the words that would become music to our ears many times over.

Todd had taken some time off from Spells, focusing on his day job and his family of six. But although his feet weren't out pounding the pavement, he couldn't turn off the ideas humming in his mind. We got together to discuss some reading he'd been doing, and to go over an important decision he'd made: he thought I had made enough progress in the lab for us to advance to the next level and establish the collaboration with RICPCom.

We met at the Flying Cow.

"I want us to set up another meeting with Joel to talk to him about the new equipment he is developing," said Todd. "I was thinking that if Nikola is still trying to bridge the size gap between her egg trays and reading plates, that maybe Joel's expertise and equipment could help fill that gap."

"I don't know, Todd," I said. "I want him to focus on being able to read the signal from our DNA samples. If it happens, then we might not need the smaller plates that Nikola's working with. Then, Nikola would not need to bridge the gap; she could use the bigger plates, and Joel's new machine could read them as is."

Todd took his time considering my point, twirling his pint glass around on the coaster in front of him.

"I see your dilemma, Scarlet," he said in that same measured tone that I always appreciated from him. "But I don't want to fall behind in this race. If Caroline and her research group at RICPCom make progress with adapting their machine and we then need to integrate Joel's, we could be working from totally useless specs. That's a lot of time and money down the drain."

"That doesn't sound good," I admitted.

"We've got to stay moving fast if we want to keep up," he said. "I know from experience working in high tech. It doesn't matter if you've poured five years of your life into a project; if they change the operating standard and your stuff doesn't fit in, that's it, you're history."

Don't shoot the messenger, I said to myself, trying to calm down about the pressure cuff of time squeezing all around me. *Todd's right. We have to find a way to work that satisfies everyone's requirements.*

"What do you suggest that we do now, then?" I asked.

"I want to see how easily we can adapt Joel's machine to work with the bigger plates and/or the smaller plates. The small ones are standard for the reading machine for 96-well plates," he offered. "I think we should also contact NavoLogic. They don't have an injection machine, so they don't have a size issue with the egg trays. Perhaps we could collaborate with them on developing the entire sexing system, injection to reading. No integration required. Then, we could dominate the market when we launch."

"We'd control the whole process then," I said.

"Exactly," he said. "Plus, I talked to Roseword about it, and he thinks we're ready."

I had been trying to keep my cool, but this felt wrong to me. That Todd would talk to our primary investor without consulting me—the one who was actually in charge of producing the technology. I tried to soften my reaction, owing to our friendship, but I could tell from the apprehensive look in Todd's eyes that he knew I was hurt.

"Todd, of course he would think we were ready," I said, pushing back. "Roseword wants a return on his investment. He doesn't care if we embarrass ourselves in the process of getting it."

I knew that it was common practice for investors to roll over their investments onto another investor. If we got an investment from NavoLogic, they could buy out Roseword's shares and he would make a profit even before our product went into production, or even if it never did.

I was suspicious of Roseword's motivations and worried that Todd was being unduly influenced by them. Maybe it was the relaxing glass of beer, maybe it was my substantial trust in Todd, or maybe it was just the maturing instinct within me to know when I truly didn't know it all. Whatever the case, I let the argument lay that night and agreed to go forward with feeling out negotiations with NavoLogic.

chapter 16

Before we parted for the night, we agreed that Todd would contact NavoLogic and set up some sort of meeting, likely by phone, as they were headquartered in France.

I was looking for some comfort, since I was, contrary to what Todd said, worried about a possible conference call with NavoLogic. Indeed, comfort was waiting: William, my newsman, was at the pub—and to my delight, with a piece of pie waiting for me.

"How's it going?" I asked as I sat down on the seat with the cinnamon apple pie in front of it. "Thanks for the pie. For me, yeah?" I asked.

"Who else?" William smiled handsomely.

I smiled back and ate my pie in silence.

"And what have you been up to?" he eventually asked.

"Not much, I am pretty exhausted today."

"Wearing yourself out buying all those new biology kits? Don't spend Roseword's money all at once." We both laughed.

I hoped he'd take charge of the conversation for a while.

"I had an interesting week," he said. "Lots of new tech out there. Everyone is blogging."

"Do you ever get any news from France?" I asked.

"France?"

"*Oui.* Do you read blogs from all over the world?"

"Yes. My searches cover everything in English, so it doesn't matter where the news is coming from. A lot of my sources are actually from Hong Kong, Singapore, places like that."

"Are the bloggers all anonymous?" I asked.

"Some are; some aren't. Some work for companies and leak inside information about a product that is about to come out, so those guys are obviously anonymous and really paranoid about being found out. Why do you ask? About France, I mean."

I told him about the conference call we were going to schedule with NavoLogic.

"A different injection company?" William asked.

"No, actually. NavoLogic doesn't have an injection machine, but they have all the other equipment and everything for the hatchery. Todd wants us to open up a line of communication with them so that we can start to build up competition among our potential buyers."

"Seems like good news to me," he said, and shrugged. "So why the long face, kid?"

"I'm not sad," I said. "Just a little overwhelmed. I feel like I have so many 'bosses' all of a sudden. I report to my angel investor. I report to someone from the injection company we're working with. And now, I may have to report with someone at NavoLogic. I also need to report to my partner, Todd, who handles the business end. And when something comes up for him, it's always an ASAP-kind of thing."

He nodded. "It's a luxury to just answer to one boss," he said, sipping his beer. "In my case, yours truly."

I sighed, playing with my fork and the few crumbs of crust left on my plate.

"I know it is a privilege that there's so much interest in our small company. I had hoped that people would be interested in what I wanted to do in the lab, but now that they are all interested, they all want to hear about my progress. And I feel I'm not progressing fast enough to have something to report about so often, you know? It's a creative process, and it takes its time."

"Ever think about blogging about your progress?" William asked with a chuckle. "Then, you wouldn't have to issue so many separate reports!"

"Oh, great," I said, "now you're laughing at my problems."

"Easy, easy," he replied with a wink. "You wanted to be popular. Now that a handful of people are interested, you're already overwhelmed. How do you think people who run giant corporations feel?"

"Honestly, William, I don't know how they do it. I have a hard time keeping things straight as it is," I said.

"You'll be fine; I have faith in you," he said.

"I wish I had your confidence."

"You might, soon enough. I have more news for you about RICPCom," he said, leaning closer and lowering his voice.

"Really?" My eyes lit up.

"Really, truly."

"Tell!"

"OK, so that thing I told you about before? It's as good as inked now," he said. "There's a huge pharma company looking to acquire RICPCom. There are serious negotiations going on as we speak."

"When are they set to sign something?" I asked.

"Well, there's a holdup," he said. "The pharmaceutical company apparently wants a chick-sexing application or, they said, the deal might be a nonstarter. They know the injection patent is about to expire, and they want something new."

"So we were right in assuming this is important," I said, a shiver of disbelief running down my spine. This was amazing news.

"Yup," he said. "Not only is it important, it might be make-or-break. It seems like RICPCom's assay isn't ready, either.

My head felt like it was swimming, and I was still as sober as a judge; the only thing I'd downed was the pie—although it had been the best I'd ever tasted. When he said, "There's one more thing," I thought I might faint.

"My sources say they'd had another product in their pipeline, which they had hoped would provide them with an edge, but I guess that fell through recently," he said.

"Did it have to do with amino acids?" I asked.

"That's what it sounded like," he said, briefly consulting some scribbled notes scratched on a steno pad. "I couldn't make heads or tails of that. What do you know about it?"

I halted, thinking of how to explain it to a layperson. But William was no ordinary nonscientist.

"Amino acids are building blocks of protein," I said, borrowing his pen and scribbling on a cocktail napkin. "If you inject certain amino acids into the egg, this prompts the chicks to then grow more rapidly while still in the egg and in the few first weeks of life. This way, they weigh more when they reach slaughtering age at six to eight weeks, and since they are sold by the pound, it becomes more profitable. I didn't like the idea of force-feeding, them in the egg, plus, if you mess around with Mother Nature, the chick may get too big and you might get fractured eggs or eggs that hatch too early. This may be a cause of death for the newly hatched chicks."

"Well, seems like your hunch about the process's flaws might be correct," he said, "because it fell through. RICPCom had sunk a lot of money into that, and it failed. And now they're desperately looking for a sexing application."

Once again, and without so much as a peck on the cheek, William had made my night. I practically floated home at the end of our encounter.

chapter 17

oel and I got straight to work and planned our experiments to see how low we could go in terms of the amount of DNA that we could detect. He joked that it was like limbo dancing.

However, for me, it was more like juggling while limbo dancing. I was now working on three projects. I was working on developing the biological reaction that would identify the sex of the chicks. Using the same idea, I was working a bit on the human project, which was a generalization of the chick sex determination. Then, I also drove every other day to Joel's lab, which was, unfortunately, half an hour away, to work on his detector.

I bought eggs for my experiments from my farmer friend, which I would then incubate for twenty-one days, drawing samples at days ten and eighteen to see if I could predict the sex. But then at three weeks, after the eggs had hatched, I had baskets full of jumping chicks on my hands. Because of agricultural laws that restricted farmers from accepting chicks that weren't incubated on their land, I couldn't bring them back to the farmer I bought them from, and I certainly wasn't going to send them to their deaths.

Instead, I found a group of farmers living off the grid, out in the woods beyond my city's limits. They were always happy to receive the chicks, but asked me how they would feed them. Sometimes, I would even see chickens around the woods and ask myself if I had checked their sex when in the egg, but I never asked the farmers what they did with the chicks, as I was so grateful that they'd accepted them.

The first time I took the eggs out of the incubator to get them ready for hatching, I prepared two shoe boxes with six separations and I put an egg in each partition. I had marked each one with a number and wanted to compare the chick's sex with the sample I had tested a few days prior in the lab to see if my predictions were right. A scientist at the veterinary institute had taught me how to carefully put a hole in the shell to reach a tiny blood vessel located on the inner side of the eggshell without touching the embryo.

On day twenty-one, I opened the incubator to find that the chicks and their feathers were still wet and they were half out of the egg. I decided I would go home to sleep and come in the next morning to drive them out to the farmers. Their feathers need to be dry for feather sexing anyhow and there was no point in driving out there at night.

When I came in the next morning, opened the incubator and looked into the shoe boxes, I found two chicks playing together in one area, three on top of each other in another part of the box, one sitting by itself in its own partition, one still struggling to get out of the shell and its friend eating the shell, trying to help it come out. It was a mess; they had jumbled themselves up to be together and I couldn't match the numbers with the chicks. The chicks seemed to be playing, warm and happy, but my experiment went kaput. I had to return to the farmer for more eggs and wait another twenty-one days.

One of the chicks was so cute, I took it home. I simply couldn't let this one go. These chicks grow so quickly, it is remarkable. In a few days it was getting so big, it was very hard to keep up with around the apartment, much less, cuddle with. It was hopping all over and making funny noises, but the best part was that as soon as I came home, it would follow me around as if I were its mother. I would go to the kitchen and it would follow me. I would go to the living room, and it would jump on the couch beside me as I sat down. At the end of the night, it would follow me to my bedroom, making a nest out of the pillow beside me. It was adorable beyond belief—so much so, that after a few days, I had trouble going to work every day because I felt guilty leaving it alone in the apartment.

After a few weeks, though, the chicken was getting too big. I knew I had to give it away, but not before I determined its sex. As I had predicted, it was a female. I took her out to the farmers in the woods and asked them to keep an eye on her and leave her for laying eggs, and they agreed not to harm her. I asked them to take care that she did not get cold at nights, as that was the most important thing to me. Then, I would visit her when I came, and she seemed happy to play outside and be free. A chicken like that can live for two to three years, happily laying eggs. I felt she was my lucky charm; I had predicted her sex correctly with my method.

Roseword suggested that for PR purposes it would help to get some local academics to act as an advisory board and support the project. Perhaps, he suggested, they'd have helpful tips as well. He was willing to pay them for their opinion, above and beyond the start-up costs he had committed to.

The first advisor that I acquired was Professor Jayson Frolev, who had responded positively from the first contact. For three hours, we just sat and geeked out over biology; I explained my work, and he was kind enough to say that he wished that all of his students were as curious as I was and were able to come up with such biotechnology. I appreciated the compliment, and it more than made up for the fact that I had been rejected by the other two professors I had approached for the advisory board. Professor Frolev agreed to read the proposal and to come to the meetings, but I was still down two advisors. I'd have to acquire those before we went much further.

chapter 18

T hings were coming along nicely after we'd received the initial investment. Todd wasted no time in getting a meeting with NavoLogic. Even though I knew how efficient he was, I was still surprised when he managed to get a conference call with the CTO in two weeks. I was overjoyed when he called me with the news.

"You're not pulling my leg?"

"I'm completely serious," he said. "And no worries about the language barrier."

I had been worried that my high school French wouldn't be up to snuff.

"Thank you so much. That's too kind of you, monsieur," I joked.

Judging by how quickly things had been moving so far, we knew from experience that two weeks would fly by all too fast. We decided to meet with Joel to loop him in as we finished and fine-tuned the material we would present on the call.

The three of us met in Joel's office. We talked over the problem of the samples being transferred from egg to plate reader with regard to size discrepancies. Joel showed us how his machine was progressing, and explained how each part had to be specifically manufactured from scratch, giving us a better idea of what might be involved if we had to change any one piece. Joel was always transparent with regards to his work and his progress and it was very comforting.

"Do you think this seems like a possibility?" I asked after everyone was through sharing their part.

Joel was thoughtful, as usual—considering his response before offering it.

"I'd have to see. If you want to cover a larger reading area, you'll need a bigger laser, and it might take more time to read the whole result," he said. "Although you might be able to read a lot more samples at a time."

I immediately went into problem-solving mode, trying to focus and solve one problem at a time.

"Do you think it would be easier to get the robotic arm to change positions or to get a bigger laser? And how would your machine fit into all this?" I asked.

He answered that if I could get him better estimates for the different sizes of the egg trays, he could perhaps give me a better idea of what we could get done.

"I'm not sure I understand though," Joel said. "If you end up needing my machine, would it really be better for you? On the one hand, we can sell this machine as is upon charging for each egg that it separates. But on the other hand, the companies might prefer a biological method they can use with already standardized equipment—less hassle for them."

"Yes, we are trying to figure that out," I conceded. "But RICPCom hasn't reached the point where they have a reliable biological test that they can use with the standard equipment, and neither have we, for that matter."

"Either way, we need to be the first to provide a solution," said Todd.

"I can get working on that estimate to see how we could customize our machine to read the egg trays." Joel said.

"Plus, if we cater to their egg-tray needs, then we should be able to maintain the lead for some time. If we manage to get our machines into the hatcheries, we will have nailed it; they will stay there for a long time," Todd said.

"I agree," I said.

"If you can get together an estimate, I will add it to our proposal," Todd told Joel, giving him the timeline for our conference call with NavoLogic.

Todd and I traveled to his house to go over our presentation. It felt good to be in a family home—a big house, big enough for his four kids to run around in. Downstairs, in the finished basement, there was an open-concept space that the kids used as a playroom, with a movie screen, a stereo system, and a library full of books, in addition to the typical toys. It contained everything a kid could need or want, I thought.

It was past their bedtime, though, so naturally, the kids were fast asleep, and the usually rowdy space was calm and quiet. In the right corner of the space was Todd's office, consisting of a desk, a chair, and a copier. The walls were decorated with lots of drawings made by his kids. His wife brought us coffee, then went back upstairs to curl up with a book and enjoy a rare moment of quiet. Then we got to work.

Todd had begun to work on an outline with his numbers and figures, but didn't want to get too ahead of things without me. I appreciated that he always waited for my input; we were equal partners. His outline included the key value proposition (chick sexing *in ovo*), the explanation of the problem, and, of course, our proposed technology. This was followed by cost projections, market potential, and our business model, followed by the scientific results and possible additional applications. Finally, there was a section marked off for concluding remarks and acknowledgments.

"How do you want to get started?" Todd asked.

"Well, let's think about our key audience, right?"

He smiled, and I knew I had gotten this right. My on-the-job business education was starting to sink in, and I had Todd and Roseword to thank for that.

"Exactly," he said. "Our audience is poultry-industry people who specialize in hatchery equipment."

"Well, let's start by telling them that we both have a vested interest in the poultry industry," I said.

Todd spoke aloud as he typed: "We're here to develop technologies to provide economic benefits to the industry, as well as improve the daily tasks of breeders through automation."

"That's good," I said, "but let's not forget: we are also thinking about the birds."

I watched Todd's fingers hover over the keys as he tried to find a way to tactfully address this subject. I knew that the birds were my passion, not Todd's. He respected that passion, but I didn't expect him to share it. He knew I wasn't going to let it go.

We wish to confront the problem of chick sexing, he wrote, highlighting the end of that slide in bright yellow, and moving on to the next slide in our presentation.

"You must admit, Todd," I said, as I watched him roll his eyes while he was typing, "that initiating the highly energy-consuming process to create a life solely for the purpose of trashing it exemplifies mankind's hubris in the most horrible way. No animal would ever do that."

One slide down, nineteen more to go. My mind had already started to wander to more comfortable places, namely, the lab. It felt so far away! I had to push through the pain of attending to the business side of things; I owed it to Todd.

"The next one is easy," I said, trying to lift myself into a more positive frame of mind. "The problem is that sorting is done manually."

"But some people don't see that as a problem," said Todd, reminding me that, all too often, businesses will just stick with what works—what has been done in the past. "So we need to tell them our motivations and goals for changing it."

"We want to automate the process, save on incubation space and electricity, and decrease the handling of chicks," I said. "The handling point is important because it just means room for spread of disease and contamination. They should like that: efficiency!"

I also made sure Todd included some cute pictures of fuzzy chicks underneath the words **HUMANE MOTIVATION** and **GO GREEN** in bold. Once we settled on a comfortable way to represent the massive killing of newborn chicks at two billion per annum, I was satisfied, and we could proceed with describing our biological assay. *Speaking of efficiency,* I thought, *wouldn't it be efficient to donate and deliver the male chicks to feed the hungry instead of letting them die and go to waste?* I knew that in some countries, they even eat cooked chicks while they are still in the egg!

We further enumerated how long the assay would take in minutes, to head off any questions about how this would affect the production process, emphasizing the high reliability and cost savings that could be shaved off the end product.

This is the solution, I wrote, believing in the mission with all my heart. *DNA.*

On to the next slide.

It got easier from there, since we proceeded to explain how we were about to achieve our technical goals and what our end product would look like. Our assay would work like a switch; light on meant female and light off meant male. The light would be read by a fluorescent reader. We did not mention anything yet about what kind of fluorescent reader would be required, not needing to complicate the explanation too much in this first meeting.

To this slide, we added what Todd thought was our most prized possession: an animated scheme of the way the assay would work. Todd had made it clear to me that business people loved animated images, and thus he invested $600 in having a graphic designer work something up for us. I have to admit, it wasn't bad; I liked it.

"We have to give them a sweet taste of the future or else they will not want to buy us," he said as he embedded the animation into the slides.

We described the constraints of alternate technologies, and again underscored how our technology was the finest of the lot. I loved the language Todd came up with for this slide: *This problem has unique characteristics that restrict the number of admissible solutions. Our approach is reliable and designed specifically for this task.*

With that kind of positive attitude and conviction, I had no doubt that Todd would make an excellent business representative for Spells. And I was learning a thing or two. With our confidence snowballing in the best possible way, we soldiered on. I made contributions where I could, and Todd did the same.

"We should probably talk about what still needs to be done, right?" I pointed to one slide.

"Great idea, Scarlet," he replied. "That way, we won't get blindsided by anything."

We knew better than to leave ourselves open to unnecessary criticism. The trick was to get people on board with Spells, not make them question us. Todd wrote down the four steps we needed to take in order to achieve the prototype: full proof of concept, development of our signal setup, sample extraction, and statistical evaluation.

I wanted to add the results here and show my lab figures, but Todd said to wait with them. They were important, but nonessential, oddly enough. Every investor we'd spoken to wanted to skip over the results section since they hadn't wanted to get into the biology; however, they had been very interested in the numbers and potential profits. Todd said we should proceed to the cost projections in accordance with the order that he had outlined.

He calculated that for the next year, we would require the sum of about $500,000 for additional human capital, including engineers, lab technicians, and another business consultant; rent for a lab; and lawyer fees. We then proceeded to his favorite two slides—Market Potential and Business Model—which included our potential collaborations and our potential end customers.

Todd inserted a table illustrating the number of laying hens worldwide, as well as the number of broilers, which he'd obtained from publicly available economic reports. He noted that if you multiply these numbers by one cent, which is the cost of manual egg sorting, you get the current cost: around $1 billion worldwide.

If you take our estimated net income for sorting each egg to be one tenth of a cent, he explained, *Spells could make at least $100 million a year. Not too shabby, I'd say.*

I then read what he had written under the title "Business Model." Under our potential collaborations he listed the three names of the hatchery automation companies, one of which, NavoLogic, we were preparing this presentation for.

As our potential end customers, he listed the four major players in the poultry industry in the United States. These were, in fact, the end consumers currently paying for the manual sorting, so they would be the ones paying for automated sorting, if it were to become available. It was amazing to me that only four companies ruled this business.

"Todd, how much would we be saving all these companies if we automated the chick sorting?" I asked.

"Well, it is a matter of interpretation because today, they pay one cent per egg for the sorting procedure. We figure we can do the assay for less than two cents per egg," he said, talking faster and faster, visibly excited by the calculations he was jotting down on a notepad for my benefit. I felt my eyes start to glaze over. Poor Todd. I started to check back in just as he reached the final figure. "The range of the game is, I would guess, somewhere around a half cent cost per egg, which means around $500 million a year can potentially be saved."

This was music to my ears, and, I hoped, to those of our future collaborators, as well.

chapter 19

was learning not to get too proud of myself for reaching milestones like we had the other night in preparing for our call. There was still so much more work to be done. Todd called me the following day; he had talked to a contact at a hatchery who had samples for us that were drawn directly from the needles injected into the eggs. We took samples for practicing against our method in the lab. I also got four new blood samples from fully grown chickens, two females and two males, taken from a vein underneath the wing. It was always a little funny to see how easy it was to take blood from the female chicken, while by contrast, the male's ego was so bruised; it would scream and shout its lungs out. Three people had to hold the male down just to draw 5 cc of blood. The females, however, were always calm and trusting.

Back at the incubator, I took the samples back into the lab and placed them in the fridge. The fridge was divided between three start-ups, and we each had our own section. We also had our own benches with closet space on top. I left the lab and waited until the next morning to start working on the samples. We added anticoagulants that do not allow the blood to clot so they would stay fresh in the fridge a few days before I processed them.

The next day, I started processing the adult blood first, which meant extracting the DNA from the blood and taking some of it for calibration purposes. My materials were expensive and I did not want to waste them, so each time before I used the blood, I did a maintenance check on it. I would amplify the signal first to make sure that it was female or male with a standard laboratory method. Then I would test mine.

I was expecting everything to be fine; I almost didn't notice the glitch. This time, the results were different from before. It showed that there were residual signs of DNA from female chickens in the male sample. This meant that my samples were contaminated, which had never happened to me before.

I was shocked. I knew it didn't happen when we took the samples, because I watched the collection with my own eyes. The tubes, the needles—everything we used was sterile and new out of the box.

What could have happened? Could anyone have touched it besides me? I was certain that none of my lab mates had touched it. We worked together in trust and respect. This is a big issue when working in a lab; we all have a sense of communal obligation to science and to one another. I felt despair and confusion and anger all at once. I repeated the test again and again, but with the same unfortunate result.

I couldn't find an explanation for the contamination, but I refused to believe it was internal to the incubator. So again, I went to the hatchery and asked the manager if I could take samples one more time. He was helpful; I apologized to him for the trouble and explained that I had to make sure the samples were good and that the first time, it did not quite work out as I had intended.

Todd and I were staring intently into the monitor of our video conference while the other end came into focus. Darrel Dubreuil, first to materialize out of the pixels on the screen, introduced himself as the CEO of NavoLogic. He sat at a small, round table that felt more like an interrogation room than a conference room—at least, from what I could see. Sitting at the table with him was the CTO, Pierre Debauchee.

On our end, it was just Todd and me in his basement office in front of our computer.

"It's so nice to meet you today, Pierre and Darrel," Todd began, making air quotes around the word *meet*. "We started this company with a singular application in mind: chick sexing. We're determined to see it through. So far, we've received investments that allow us to do the work as frugally as possible, taking very low salaries and using most of the funding for rent, equipment, and essentials. We are very close to a proof of concept, and we estimate it will take us two years to reach a prototype."

This was met with a stony silence.

Todd continued, "If you will allow us, we have a presentation to show you."

"Yes, please do," said Dubreuil. "And you. You are the young mademoiselle Todd spoke of on the phone, correct?"

I nodded, scooting a little closer to the camera.

"It's your idea to use the DNA to sort the chicks?"

"Yes, sir, in a new specific way" I said, trying to convey confidence but not cockiness. "I believe it is the best way to reach definitive results. DNA does not lie."

"*Oui*. It would be wonderful, I think, to have something you can check without invading the egg," he said.

"I wish I could think of a way to make that happen," I said. "But without injecting anything into the egg or extracting any samples, I don't see how that can be done. The sex organs are too small to recognize with ultrasound, and you'd have to check them one by one anyway; multisampling is surely preferred to save time."

I played dumb, not mentioning that I had heard about their heartbeat method. I wanted to see if he would tip his hand. In the background, Todd had finished setting up the presentation. I turned it over to him. We had planned that he would talk until we came to the lab results, and that I would carry on from there. I loved listening to Todd talk business; he was a pro for sure. He could truly sell ice to the Inuit.

When the animated scheme of the method played through, Debauchee said he was quite impressed by what he viewed to be a genuinely innovative method.

"Yes, sir," I answered. "I am now in the process of narrowing down the search for the sequences, which appear multiple times in the chicken genome. This will allow for producing a repetitive signal, which, in turn, will provide enough amplification to acquire a signal within the required resolution."

"Interesting," said Debauchee, considering further implications. "If you have such a method, it can be used to identify other species as well, yes?"

"Correct. Repetitive units—in other words, *sequences*—are frequent in every living organism, and they are usually unique to that species. These sequences are now being determined by genome-sequencing projects, which can provide useful information of repetitive sequences for detection by our method," I said.

"Tell me then," Debauchee continued with his line of inquiry, "if you have a way of detecting species in low quantities and in non-lab settings, why have you started with the chick-sexing application? What about medical biodiagnostics? There's a lot of money there."

I tried to channel all the advice I'd gotten from Todd, all of the confidence and fierceness that he displayed in his deft handling of negotiations.

"That's an interesting question, Mr. Debauchee," I admitted. "We're passionate about this application. You can certainly understand the utility, correct?"

I was trying to dig for information without really saying so. I hoped that Debauchee would admit either that their company was, or was not, trying to pursue the solution to this problem, themselves.

Dubreuil may have sniffed this out, because he cut back into the conversation.

"Pierre is always full of interesting questions," he said, imbuing the air with a slight degree of tension.

Todd continued with the presentation, and I tried to smile, though not while Todd was talking. I would occasionally sip from a glass of ice-cold water, letting it slide past the lump that was forming in my throat. I hoped my gulping wasn't obvious.

When Todd got to the Market Potential slide, Dubreuil asked, "There are 130 billion eggs produced worldwide?"

"Yes, sir." Todd answered. "This data comes from the latest industry economic-trends reports."

"What happens if you don't convince the whole world to use your machine? Who do you think you can get for sure, and how much would that be worth per year?" Dubreuil asked, putting on the pressure, turning up the heat.

"Well, as you may have guessed, we are talking to companies with the required injection equipment. Those companies have connections to the poultry-processing companies, which I'll actually list on the following slide," said Todd.

"I see. So you're assuming penetration into the US market?"

"Absolutely. As you can see, that adds up to a large profit per year," Todd said. "I wanted to ask—if you don't mind sharing—do you have information on the European market? What are the numbers like over there?"

"I'm sure we can get that information for you, can't we, Pierre?" asked Dubreuil.

Debauchee nodded. I tried my hardest to read their facial expressions, but alas, they were inscrutable.

"So you said you've been speaking with the egg-injection companies too, then?" asked Dubreuil.

"Yes," confirmed Todd. "But we're keeping our options open, as you can see."

We skipped through the Results section faster than I would have liked. Debauchee, in addition to being the company's chief technology officer, was a veterinarian by trade, and said that he preferred that someone on his research team with a more specific background in molecular bio take a more in-depth look at our materials. When we finished the presentation, they both smiled and nodded to one another.

"To be honest, we're actually looking to set up a research-and-development group in molecular biology," shared Debauchee. "This would take on three projects at most, one of which would be chick sexing. We have looked at other potential solutions to this issue and we are considering where to put our funds. Perhaps we will invest in more than one method."

"This is good news," I said.

"It is good news, indeed," said Debauchee, "because I very much liked what I saw here today! I think we can collaborate with you and give you the information you've requested. We will monitor your progress, and perhaps we will be able to make you an offer of sorts in the near future. Let's agree to stay in touch. Is this OK by you?"

"Certainly," Todd replied, "We look forward to it. Thank you again for giving us the opportunity to show you our work."

We all said our good-byes, and Todd switched off the camera.

"It was a good meeting," he said. "It definitely ended on a positive note."

I agreed with him, but I had to admit, I was a little disappointed. After all the buildup, I was expecting more commitment from them. If Debauchee was going to set up a molecular-biology lab and was checking out prospective projects, and he'd liked our work, what had stopped him from making an offer to us right there and then? Why wait?

was still mulling over the call when Lauralynn called to ask if I wanted to accompany her to a party that evening.

"There are going to be lots of interesting folks there," she said. "Maybe some people you'd hit it off with for Spells. Plus, you've been working so hard, you can probably use the distraction!"

I was quite thankful for the invitation and I didn't hesitate.

I had made a conscious decision to really let loose that night, and I was so glad I did. The party was a blast; delicious barbeque and cakes towered over tables, while the fine wine flowed like water and everyone was dressed to the nines.

Lauralynn got a kick out of introducing me to her friends.

"Have you met Scarlet? She's the chick sexy girl!" she'd say, and guffaw at their reaction. People always wanted to know more. "You can come to my office and pay $376 an hour to hear more about it."

I was all for it; I loved to talk about my research, after all. But such an introduction probably would make them think they were in for a very different explanation.

I learned pretty quickly that I was rubbing elbows with the elites of our city's society. There was the scion of the real-estate entity, a tall and curly young man, just out of school, having finished his master's degree and looking to obtain a Ph.D. in a scientific field. His father, who owned the highest skyscraper in the city (among many other properties), had sent him to the party to sniff out potential investment opportunities. Another real-estate tycoon talked my ear off about the four Jaguars he owned, his hotels, and his various properties. He also had a lot of patents, as he bought them as investments.

"If yours is for sale," he said, looking me up and down, "I'll gladly buy it."

He toasted me with a glass of wine, and told me his name, although I just thought of him as Bob the Apartment King, on account of the various apartments he claimed to own throughout the city. ("Just put your finger on a map, and I've got one nearby. Come and visit.") He gave me his business card and said he had a lead on some warehouse and lab spaces for rent; I thought that might be useful, so I slid it into my clutch.

"Let me know if you reconsider about that patent," he said.

It was an exciting night and a great crowd. I think Lauralynn had met most of the people she knew there on social networks. I caught myself wondering if anyone there knew William. While I was dancing to some '80s pop, I looked across the room and locked eyes with none other than Roseword.

"Hey, what are you doing here? Shouldn't you be in the lab?" he asked, smiling. He seemed more relaxed than I'd ever seen him before.

"Oh, sure, that's all I do," I said, playfully mocking him. "I'm in the lab 24/7. Hey, did Todd give you the good news?"

"Yeah, he gave me the short version and said he'd expand on it in our next meeting. He said he hoped he'd have more to report by then," said Roseword. "How is work going?"

"It is fine, progressing," I answered, reminding myself of something that I realized I'd rather forget.

"Would you mind if I took her away for a few minutes?" he asked the guy who had been my dance partner. We walked away from the dance floor, after he'd excused himself from the woman with whom he was dancing, and sat down at one of the tables.

"So, really, what are you doing here? Don't you have a boyfriend waiting at home?"

"Don't you have a wife waiting at home?" I asked, being a little rude.

"I guess we never actually got into the details of our private lives, huh?"

"Not really," I said. "But I did see your son when we were over at your house."

"If you must know," he said, "I'm divorced. But we do have one child. He's ten."

"Well, since we're sharing, I'm single, no kids. Some chicks running around here and there."

"Interesting," he said. "Young, talented person like you? I'd think you would have someone."

I tried not to blush, and that only made me blush harder.

"Actually, I do have someone whom I'm kind of seeing on a somewhat regular basis," I said. *If one night a week is considered a "somewhat regular basis,"* I thought to myself. *And if "seeing" is literally just sharing a beer and a slice of pie with.*

We talked a little more about what we did in our downtime. He participated in triathlons to keep in shape. I talked about the chicks that I'd taken from the farm, and admitted that I hadn't had much time to work out lately, although I had just recently joined a gym.

"I'm a little tense about NavoLogic," I admitted.

Suddenly, he didn't seem to want to talk about work at all.

"No shop talk," he said, shaking his head. "Enjoy some barbecue. Finish your margarita." The conversation took another turn; he solicitously invited me out to come with him on his yacht someday, take a break from the lab. I sensed that he might be flirting with me, and I wasn't sure how to feel about it. On the one hand, I enjoyed the attention; on the other, I felt it was inappropriate and I questioned his motives.

I decided that since we'd both let our guard down, I would gently poke fun at this.

"You know, I might start to think that you didn't invest in our project solely for your concern over the painful deaths of newborn chicks," I teased.

"I did it for the money," he said, "and I believe you'll come through with the product."

Good, he was understanding the boundaries I was setting.

"So you believe in me?"

"I've believed you can do anything you set your mind to do, since the first time I saw you," he said in a serious tone before turning on a dime. "Although, a young woman thinking she can change the world, it's a little naïve, albeit romantic." I must have made a face; he could tell my feelings were hurt. "Don't get defensive," he said. "I'm just dishing it back out. Seriously though. This is going to be hard, Scarlet."

I felt my jaw start to tense. If I were a cat, my hackles would be raised.

"You're aware who you're taking on, right?" he asked. "There are big corporations who have a vested interest in keeping things as they are, as they have been for years. How are you going to change their minds?"

"We'll play them against each other," I said. "They'll all want a chick-sorting solution."

"But that is only true for the injection-device companies. Do the poultry corporations need it?" he asked. "Could they do without it?"

"I guess they could," I admitted. "They have been. But I assume they'll just buy whatever the injection companies sell them. If one corporation has a chick-sorting solution, the other one will want it too, so all the injection company has to do is to have them compete with each other in order to get them to sign on. On the other hand, you're right that if the injection machine no longer existed, they could just go back to manual injection and not miss it."

"So they are being sold something that they can essentially do without?" he pushed.

"But automation means progress, and that is why they agreed to it in the first place. It must have saved them money," I pushed back.

"I don't know, Scarlet," he said. "Still seems a little more of a romantic idea than a strictly monetary issue."

I felt my jaw start to tense up again, and knew he must have seen it.

"But to be completely honest, that's part of why I wanted to invest."

"So you're a little romantic yourself, huh?"

"Maybe I do care about those newborn chicks," he said. "Especially since they're all male. That's just cruel."

"In all seriousness, Roseword," I said, wanting to make my point, now that I felt he'd be receptive. "It's that kind of thought—the 'strictly business' thought—that hinders progress. I was raised to think about ideals, about making the world a better place. If you put a price tag on everything, it makes it hard to do that."

"You're right, and that's exactly why I invested in you. Who knows, maybe you will turn me into a believer, after all," he said.

"Who knows, maybe you can turn me on to biking, running, and swimming," I shot back.

"Cheers to that." We raised our wineglasses.

"Say," he began, a sly smile taking over his face, "have you ever had *Kürtöskalács?*

"Never."

"There's a great bakery right around the corner and they make the best ones you'll ever taste. Ever," he said.

I said a quick good-bye to Lauralynn, and the two of us snuck out of the party.

It turned out to be an amazing cake.

"Have you ever tasted Taiwanese brioche?" I asked him as I munched away.

"Brioche is French."

"You would think so, but if you tasted the Taiwanese brioche that I tasted, you would change your mind. I have a friend whose uncle owns a bakery in Taiwan and each time she goes there, she brings one back for me; it melts in your mouth," I gushed.

"We could fly there tonight and taste it if you'd like," he said, enjoying his cake.

"No, I'm OK with this, thanks" I said. "Besides, right now, I have way too much work to do. But I will definitely take a rain check."

chapter 22

We finally got around to arranging a biology bench in one of the corners of the open space at Joel's office, and we set up a miniature refrigeration and freezer unit. This would save me the time and effort of traveling back and forth with the materials and tubes, carrying everything in ice buckets in my car. This way, I could take half days and work with Joel longer on developing that aspect of the application.

We bought all the necessary equipment: pipettes, a tube shaker, a temperature block, *etc.* Luckily, since we were not yet working with biological samples, we did not require special security measures. It was more or less suitable for what we needed. It was garage-style, true, but it would do. The only real hassle was getting insurance in case something happened to me.

Initially, we thought we'd put me on Joel's insurance policy because I was working at his building and they had insurance for everyone under their roof. However, this was only for workers or visitors, and I was neither; I worked for Spells. After some finagling, I was able to write Joel under the Spells insurance policy at no additional cost and we added me on as a volunteer at Joel's company, which oddly, conferred insurance.

With those logistics out of the way, I went to see William at the pub. I wanted to tell him about the talk with Debauchee and Dubreuil. He was sitting at our usual table, waiting for me. He never missed a date, and neither did I, even though we didn't communicate ahead of time to schedule it. I still didn't have his phone number or contact information of any kind. Maybe he's here every night, I thought. Maybe I should come more often.

"*Bonsoir, ma chérie,*" William greeted me as I sat down.

"*Je ne parle pas français,*" I joked. I thought it was pretty witty, saying I don't speak French in French.

"Oh, I thought that since you had the meeting with NavoLogic, you would be fluent by now. How did it go?" He smiled.

I shrugged. "Todd thinks it went well, but we didn't close a deal. They agreed to collaborate and wait to monitor our progress, much like RICPCom."

"Perhaps they feel the timing is a little premature. Maybe if you show them some more progress, they will invest," William reassured me.

"I don't know. The CTO specifically said he was searching for projects to invest in and take under his wing," I said.

"Aren't these the people working on the heartbeat solution?" William asked.

"Ostensibly," I said, "but neither one of the people we met with would give us any information on that application or where it stands."

"Did they say anything about your method, besides agreeing to collaborate?" William asked.

"They complimented us on the method, but they still weren't ready to make a commitment," I said, frustrated.

"Well, you still have money to work right? Take your time and work. The more progress you make on your own, the more you will be worth when they decide they want you," William pointed out.

"I guess you're right," I said. "Maybe I'm expecting the wrong things from these meetings. I guess I'm looking for confirmation when what I should really be looking for is information. I should be thinking of them as future customers, and I need to find out from them what type of product they need."

"Now you're talking," said William. "Although, I'd hate for you to have to move to France so soon after we've met."

Soon? I thought to myself. *Boy, this guy is slow-moving.*

"Oh, don't worry about that. I won't be moving anywhere for now," I said with a wink. "I have a lot of work to do. I don't know what is with this bar, but my eye is bothering me again. Would you be so kind as to check it again?" I leaned close to him.

He checked it, putting on a very serious face and then said with a wink, "You're fine. Nothing to worry about."

"Thanks, I always get worried because I once worked with this guy who had a simple eyelash caught in his eye and it scratched his cornea. He was in terrible pain," I said, trying to explain my quirkiness. "William, please tell me a bit more about yourself," I said, sitting back down across from him. "I really want to know *you* better, we always talk about me and my business."

"Sure, ask me anything. I'm game to answer."

"Well, like, what's your favorite color?"

"Ooh, such a hard question," he said, giving me a hard time. "I'll go with blue. Yours?"

"I like orange. I think blue goes perfectly with orange, don't you?" I teased.

"Mmm-hmm. OK, I get the drift; I'll tell you more about myself. I consider myself a level-headed, down-to-earth kind of guy. I love life and long walks on the beach, and I am usually totally immersed in the woman I love. I'm very devoted, you know."

"But first you need to *be* in love . . ." I was fishing for answers.

"I tend to come across as shy, but I open up at the right time and with the right person. I am generally calm, confident, and happy. I do admit I am an introvert by nature. I'm organized; I like a lot of structure."

"I guess you would have to be organized in order to be a journalist and own your own business. I try to be extremely organized in the lab, unlike in my personal life and my apartment," I said, laughing.

"I love to show attention, but sometimes I have a pretty awkward sense of humor and people may see it as more of a tease or a test than being funny. So I tend to stay friends with those who stick around despite my humor or those who just like it kinky. I look at it this way: I'd rather make a joke than sit around and dwell on things I can't do much to change."

"I don't know, I can take a joke as long as the context and timing is right, but I have noticed there is sometimes a fine line between a joke and a put-down and that's where I have learned to draw the line. I am too sensitive, I cry profusely in movies, and I cry at books or sometimes even about notes people write. So sometimes jokes offend me, even though I always prefer a man with a sense of humor to a man without."

"I will try to be sensitive around you, Scar, so as not to leave a scar in your heart. I see you for the beautiful soul you are, Scarlet. A woman's beauty is seen in her eyes, it's the doorway to her heart and I find you to be very beautiful. I want to keep you safe." He held my hand, looked into my eyes and became very quiet all of a sudden. As he was pondering, a cloud of grave concern passed over his face. "I wanted to tell you something," he said, lowering his voice as he usually did when he was about to drop a bomb. "Watch out for your new guy. Joel, I think you said his name was?"

I didn't understand why he was bringing Joel up.

"Yes, Joel. Why?"

"Just watch out for his safety. It's just a hunch."

I felt a lump start to rise in my throat, a knot start to twist in my stomach. I realized I didn't know William very well at all. Was he just messing with my head? Was this his twisted sense of humor that he was talking about? It couldn't be. I nodded at him, deciding to call it a night shortly after that. It took me hours to find sleep, and when I did, it was fitful.

chapter 23

One of the blessings—though sometimes, it was a curse—about the incubator space was that it wasn't just me and my equipment. One day, an investor walked into the lab, looking classy in a white satin suit and flanked by an accountant. It turned out, he was investing in the company that worked beside me; they were working on diagnosing the level of antibiotics in milk. He was satisfied with a meeting they'd just had and was clearly in a good mood, so he introduced himself.

"I'm Lenny Yang," he said. "And what is it you're doing?"

His ears perked up when I started in on my simple pitch: "Chickens."

I told him a little bit about it, not in great detail, but I was excited by the opportunity to talk with an investor, right there in the lab without having to dress up and go to a meeting in a fancy office space. He asked me to send him my presentation and said he would like to meet with me again. Of course, I immediately called Todd and Roseword and told them the good news.

A short time later, Roseword offered that we meet on his yacht, but Mr. Yang preferred that we come to his house to talk.

So Roseword sent Todd, Joel, and me to meet this investor at his home. We drove over to his house and found it to be a sprawling affair with many rooms. He invited us to sit down in the living room, but

Todd asked for a place where he could show his presentation. Lenny assured us that he felt more comfortable in the living room and that Todd could explain everything he needed without slides.

Todd began explaining but Lenny cut him off; there was a story he had to tell us about a woman who gave birth in a car when he was on one of his trips to Africa. He just *had* to tell it to us, he said, since we were on the subject of pregnancy. He finished the story as Joel was finishing the bowl of macadamia nuts on the table, pointing out that he had never before considered laying eggs as a *pregnancy* per se.

Todd went on to describe the equipment Joel had been working on for the last four years. Again, Lenny cut him short.

"If we're talking about Africa," he said, "I've been to Mount Kilimanjaro. Boy, do I have a story about that."

Lenny told us about how he took his seven-year-old son there, proclaiming that if you can take a few hours' flight to Africa to see the animals in the wild, why would you take the kids to the zoo in the nearby town? If you include traffic and the crowds, he reasoned, it is more worth your while to fly to Africa than drive to the local zoo.

After he took his kids to see the animals, they went on to explore Mount Kilimanjaro. They started climbing the mountain with a guide and suddenly, his son became blue, experiencing shortness of breath. Lenny hadn't known what had happened or what to do. Had he swallowed something?

Lenny called the paramedics with a walkie-talkie and they had to climb the mountain to meet them. His son had a case of mountain sickness, which meant the mountain air was too thin for him. The child started vomiting as well. In this case, they said, he would not be able go higher until the symptoms disappeared and that he should stay put until he felt better. They also reprimanded him for taking the kid with him on the climb. They camped there and climbed down the next morning.

Lenny explained that it was not a big deal though because he flew there every other weekend, and that someday his son would be able to climb the famous mountain. He invited us to come along some time.

"I take excellent photos of the animals," he bragged.

Then he let Joel talk about the things he wanted to add to his machine and how much money it would take. But then suddenly, Lenny remembered that he had wonderful pictures of his adventures in Africa that we might be interested in seeing. Of course, we were; we couldn't very well turn him down in his own home. He took us down to his office and showed us slides on his new wide-screen, using his brand-new projector, and we saw him climb Mount Kilimanjaro, which is, he emphasized, the highest mountain in Africa and the highest "walkable" mountain in the world.

Todd suggested that since we were already in his office and we had the slide projector switched on, he could maybe use it to show Lenny the presentation. Joel also wanted to show a short video about how the machine was built and works.

"That'll be fine," said Lenny. "But first, maybe we can take a look at these pictures. Personally, they're almost professional grade. I should skip this whole thing and get a job with *National Geographic.*"

We tried to muster a chuckle. And indeed, his pictures were impressive. He told us that he'd spent all night in a jeep waiting to get a close-up of the lions since he'd had the finest cameras and lens to achieve a fantastic shot.

"The technology is cutting-edge," he said. "I have people inside the industry and I can acquire these things before the general public sees them."

Since Lenny seemed to be genuinely intrigued by cutting-edge technology, Joel tried to tell him that we might be selling our technology soon.

"You can get a first look before it's sold," he said. "And maybe get in on a piece of the action.

Lenny was intrigued enough to hear more, so he took us into his studio, where he had reproduced his photographs into posters of different sizes. I began explaining the application, and then he picked up one poster of a chicken. He said he had taken it on one of his trips to the poor farms in Africa, where they had nothing but a few chickens. He thought to himself that he had seen thousands of chickens in his life so why would he need a picture of this one? But something had made him take it.

"Now I know why," he said. "It's for you. A gift. You should hang it on a wall wherever you continue your project."

While he said the chicken photo was a gift, he wanted to sell us another to cover the cost of his framing. We agreed, and Lenny thrust two more framed posters into Todd's hand as he showed us to the door and asked us for $400.

Surprisingly, we were the ones who were writing the check at the end of this meeting.

"I will call a friend of mine, who works with entrepreneurs, like yourselves, to bring about their ideas into products. He will be happy to meet with you, and I, too, will think about what you've said."

"He's a great salesman," said Todd once we were back in the car.

chapter 24

was beginning to feel stretched thin. I had meetings to go over the patent work and every few days, I received e-mails I needed to jump on for Nikola at RICPCom. Joel, meanwhile, wanted us to conduct a meeting every two weeks to go over the details of our progress with his investors. Todd thought we should meet more often at the Flying Cow to discuss business strategy. And Roseword's partner, Samuel Cole, was e-mailing me every so often to ask for an update on how things were going. I could not refuse any e-mail inquiry or meeting request that came my way.

Between attending all these meetings and talking about the work that I should be doing, how could I be expected to actually *get that work done?* On top of that, I had the newsman more and more frequently on my mind. Not just his handsome face, but also the news that he had let slip about the potential merger. What could it mean for us if the injection company merged with a huge pharmaceutical player? I thought I should talk about it with Todd, but wondered if that would betray William's trust. I felt like I needed to ask his permission.

To my relief, Todd was helpful in other ways, too; he was handling the talks with NavoLogic for now so I did not have to report to them, as I did to Nikola. I was still a little disappointed that they could not make us an offer of some sort, but with all that was up in the air right now, it came as a bit of a relief anyway.

"I haven't the faintest idea what I would do if they made us an offer, Todd," I said. "I'm not ready to sell. I still have work to do."

Todd had a far-off look in his eyes.

"And we can't take the chance that they may buy it just to bury it," he said, something clicking deep inside his mind.

"Do you really think they would do that?"

"Sure," he said. "Especially if they're progressing with the heartbeat method, they would want to bury the competition. I have no idea how far they've come with it; they won't even mention it."

"Well, if they talk about buying in the future, we would need to see that the project proceeds under certain contract constraints," I said. He nodded approvingly.

"If they do make us an offer, at this stage, I think we are talking 5 to $10 million. However, if you find the chicken genome sequence you're looking for, then we could be worth a whole lot more."

"Definitely, because we could sell that as a trade secret and that would make it almost impossible to reproduce and copy, even when the patent on our method expires."

"What are you waiting for, kiddo?" he said, smiling. "Get a move on!"

He was trying to lighten the mood, but suddenly, I felt heavier than ever. It was dawning on me how much pressure was on me, how if I didn't get the sequence and they bought us to bury us first, I'd never forgive myself. Tears started to well up in my eyes; I tried to hide this from Todd, but he saw them just before they started to fall.

"Scarlet," he said softly, as reassuring as I imagined he was with his children, "it'll be all right. We won't do anything you don't feel comfortable doing. Remember, you still own the majority of the shares."

I sniffled. "I'm suddenly so happy about that fact," I said, trying to smile.

I thought for a moment.

"Would you consider moving to France and continuing the project there?"

Todd laughed. "Are you nuts?! We aren't all free spirits like you, Scarlet. I've got kids in school."

He watched my face and could tell that I wasn't kidding.

"On the one hand, I would just like to continue working where I do now, but on the other, if they form a research group where everybody is working on poultry-related ideas, it would be a productive environment for me to work in, not to mention the resources I would probably have," I said.

"We're getting ahead of ourselves, kiddo. Let's think about the pros and cons when and if we get an offer," he said.

As I tried to stop my mind from spinning a million miles ahead, something crept into a dark corner of my consciousness: the one person I'd miss terribly if I moved away. My news guy. *Well,* I thought, *he is hardly* my *news guy.* I didn't even have his phone number. For all I knew, he could be a married man.

To experience a change of pace, I decided that I would call Bob, the Apartment King, to get a tour of the available warehouses in town, and he was happy to oblige me. *Maybe, just maybe, we would need to expand a little,* I thought. I had always loved real estate, particularly open spaces—so much potential! It was a real treat.

Bob drove us around little streets in town and walked us through the local market area. He pointed at one building, and then another, and announced he had apartments in both. I asked him how he remembered it all and he said that he'd bought almost all of them himself; he remembered where his hard-earned money had gone.

We arrived at an area with factories, saloons, auto dealerships, and garages. Bob took me into some of the factories. Unfortunately, a lot of them were empty spaces, as either the factories had moved out of the city to get cheaper rates or had shut down because everything now was imported from the Far East. He said that the rent was not too bad around there, and that he could get us a good deal if I found something I liked.

He explained that that area was slowly turning into a creative corridor for artists of all kinds. The artists had realized they could rent out old warehouses and turn them into a place where they could create their art and live, loft-style, at the same time. Customers could visit easily, and the workshops were centrally located.

"Is the deal only for artists?"

"Kind of," Bob explained. "There's a special government subsidy for them in the area."

My face started to fall; I was getting so excited about these spaces.

"But," he said, "now that I think of it . . . aren't you a kind of artist? You work with biological materials. You play around with them to create a product. Sounds like an artist to me."

"Yes, but the product has nothing to do with aesthetics."

"But it represents a moral issue! Art tries to convey a moral message. My point is that if you could get an artist permit, I could rent it out to you on the cheap," said Bob, trying to be helpful.

"I guess it's worth a try," I said.

We walked through the alleyways, peeking into different workshops. We walked into one space which had beautiful pottery in various stages of completion lining the floor and shelves. It was a large, open space with little stools, a ceramic bowl placed on each one. The colors that dominated were black, brown and Skobeloff green, giving the space a calm, natural vibe. Bob introduced me to the owner, Tao.

"How are you enjoying being here, Tao?" I asked.

"It's pretty good," he said. "Business is slowly picking up, more and more people are starting to become aware of this place, and they come to look and shop."

Tao showed us his public space as well as his room in the back, where he worked on private projects out of the public eye. He said that he could help explain the process of getting the artist permit, if I wanted. I was all too eager to hear about it, and he asked me what I would be working on.

"If I got a place like this, I would probably bring over a few chickens so I could have eggs every morning, and I would install an incubator," I said. "I think it would fit in well in an artist colony, to have a few chickens running around. What do you think?"

Tao laughed. "At least then we're sure to get fresh eggs every day. It would certainly add to the unique atmosphere of this place."

As we walked around the space, I saw a captivating sculpture coming up from the floor. Tao caught my inquisitive gaze.

"That's my crushed man," he offered.

"What?"

"I had started to make a sculpture of a man out of clay, but after I had finished, it slipped through my fingers and dropped to the ground. Half of him flattened; the other half was fine. I thought I'd leave him here like this."

"I will take him!" I said, "Maybe I can take him home and, with a lot of patience and care, make him whole again."

"I wouldn't try too hard," he said. We continued with the tour and I saw very beautiful and extraordinary ceramics; Tao had good hands.

He took us into his neighbor Tammy's rug shop. Tammy was a thin, red-haired girl who hand-tufted rugs by pulling yarn through holes in a primary backing, eventually creating, in this case, decorative wall hangings. Tammy worked with a painter across the street to make rugs from his paintings, adding the yarn tufts in accordance with the painter's colors. If you wanted the original painting, you could go over to the painter's shop across the street and buy it.

Listening to the artists talk about their process, I felt a familiar itch in my hands. That feeling of needing to go back to the lab and pipette. I loved working with my hands; and the rhythmic motion would relax my mind and send me to a better place. I would put tubes in front of me and pipette, just putting ten microliters of this or that into each tube, depending on the experiment. I could understand the feeling of sitting and weaving all day, it was heaven—or at the very least, occupational therapy.

After leaving Tammy, Bob took me to the final warehouse space, and like Goldilocks, I felt that this one was *just right*. *If I could only rent it, I would put my lab bench right here,* I thought. *We could make room for Joel's equipment over there. The back room could be used for the incubator. We could get a lab-grade injection machine from RICPCom so that I could use it to practice extracting samples from eggs. We could then grow them into chickens right here, as no one would be disturbed by it, with all the grass in the back.*

There was another small room, which I could use as an office and a couple of rooms upstairs. We could paint it the way we wanted and decorate it with the local artwork from the shops in the courtyard!

I felt dizzy with possibility. With everything in place, and with some new machinery, I could do things so much faster and we would have that prototype running in no time. I would run that machine day and night to do all my testing. As it stood now, I needed to drive to the facility to use it and I would take all my tubes there in the car, on ice, to get there. If I could just have everything in one place, the ideal working space, what a dream come true it would be! In a way, I already felt very much like an artist, at least in my soul and in my dreams.

After I parted ways with Bob, my spirits felt so lifted and I was hopeful that maybe one day I would be able to rent a space like the ones I saw that day.

I made my way to the pub, hoping to see William. There he was, waiting in a booth with a slice of warm pie. He warmed my heart.

"Did you mention you were in touch with RICPCom when you talked to the NavoLogic guys?" he asked as I sat down, ready to dig in.

"Good evening to you too," I said. "You know, I love your beautiful eyes, I just have to mention it real quick."

He smiled and looked down.

"Back to the topic at hand. Yes, we did. We wanted to get their reaction."

"And what was it?" he asked tensely.

I had been so happy just a moment ago, but now something was clearly going on that was bigger than my earlier excursion through the artist colony.

"They didn't seem surprised. Maybe they expected they wouldn't be the first ones we approached," I said. "And, you know, Todd pointed out that they may want to buy us just to bury us."

"Someone may be interested in burying it, but I am not sure it is them," he said, his voice lowering to a gravelly whisper.

"What do you mean by that?" I was surprised, and I'd lost any semblance of an appetite. I set down my fork, a perfect bite of pie still on its tines.

"I'm not sure. I need to investigate it further," he said. "But what I do know is that you may have caused a stir in the poultry world. Influential people are not so interested in seeing your solution come to fruition."

My blood ran cold. I opened my mouth to speak, then thought better of it. I should let William do the talking.

"You know the story of David and Goliath?" he asked.

I nodded, then gulped. I was so looking forward to share my good day with William, and suddenly I felt sad. The ups and downs of research were something I was used to. One day, you're up and things are going well; the next day, you're down and your spirits fall. You are at the whims of your research; it was much like being under a spell.

This was the first time I experienced feeling the ups and downs of the business world. I could only hope William was mistaken, but he seldom was.

"OK," I said, rubbing my eye hard. "Sorry, now I *just know* I have something in my eye. I am sure it's an eyelash; can you check? Just to be sure?" I leaned in toward him.

"Nope, all clear," he said reassuringly after checking, holding back a laugh.

"What? It can be very dangerous, seriously, eyelashes getting caught in your eye." I cried out.

"Yes, Scar, I don't doubt it, sweetheart," he said, trying to maintain a serious face for me.

Oh-em-gee, I thought. *He just called me 'sweetheart.'* My heart skipped a beat.

chapter 25

What William had said bothered me more than I wanted to admit. It rang in my ears as I was falling asleep, and it was the first thing I thought of when I woke up the next day. I had expected we might face some resistance, but I was genuinely surprised to think that it would come to threats.

I decided I had to meet Caroline and Nikola at RICPCom, thinking perhaps that I could get their reassurance face-to-face. Todd agreed, especially since we hadn't gotten anywhere with NavoLogic. Todd set up the meeting at a hotel and we were scheduled to fly there in two days. Then, I received a strange call from Cole, Roseword's partner.

Cole and I sat down to a meeting at a coffee shop close to his office. I was surprised he'd called and asked to meet me alone, but I couldn't have refused. Of course, my curiosity had gotten the better of me.

"Hi, my dear. How are you? It is nice to meet with you again," Cole said.

I was immediately turned off; he talked as though he was twenty years older than me, when he was probably a couple of years younger. He was arrogant, with a false sense of accomplishment, I reasoned.

"I wanted to talk to you about Spells today, even though I don't tend to interfere in Roseword's private business and in our investment firm, as you know, we mainly focus on disruptive innovations. Mostly in cleantech, of course, although we're in other sectors as well."

"Yes, I know all that, I am interested to know why you called me here today," I said, trying to cut him off as his very first words still rang in my ear. How could any one person be so annoying?

He continued, ignoring my urgency: "I must emphasize to you the importance of Roseword and his accomplishments. I don't know if you have read about him, but he has achieved great things in his career."

I had no idea where this was leading, and raised my eyebrows accordingly.

"So you can understand that we do not want to do anything that would tarnish his reputation—one which has taken him years of schooling and working to achieve," he continued.

"And?"

"You are not a fool, Scarlet, we have serious venture capital backers and other companies that we work with who require Roseword's full attention. We are working on building an empire. Many people depend on him and yet, all he's focusing on these days is your petty chick problem. I don't know what kind of web you have spun him into, but I will have you know, there are people who will go to great lengths to put an end to Spells," he said sternly.

"Honestly, Cole, I do not spin webs around men," I said, with a roll of my eyes that I could not contain. "I believe Roseword is a grown man who makes his own decisions and can fend for himself. Beyond that, this is just business, and I resent you implying anything more. Here I was, foolishly thinking you wanted to meet me to offer more help to Spells. But instead, you're here to threaten me?! You are not half the man Roseword is."

I was spitting fire at the gall of this man. I don't know why I always fall into the trap of thinking the best of people.

"Scarlet, I am here to warn you that there are things beyond your knowledge or your control at play," he said. "You started this thing and therefore, you must end it. You are a talented young woman and I will find you a job in another firm, I know. You will be well compensated and taken care of; don't worry."

"Mr. Cole, I am not interested in doing any other work than lab work. I love my job! It is what keeps me going. What's *really* bothering you? Stop being so elusive and tell me directly what's wrong."

"I am not your friend, Scarlet. Don't push me."

He leaned back in his chair and looked away from me.

"I am sorry," I said. "I act on reason, not simply to comply blindly, and if you have something to explain to me, I want the details so I can make up my own mind about what to do."

"Sometimes it's wise to listen to people who have your back."

I did not smile. "You just told me you're not my friend."

"I am not your enemy, either, Scarlet," he said. "I need you to do what I ask for the sake of Roseword's whole identity. Shut down Spells, find another project to work on. You are young; you'll have other ideas. There's still much to learn."

"To my understanding, Roseword represents kindness, as well as clear, progressive, common sense thinking. He is not arrogant and fake like the people who work for him, thinking they can push anyone around," I said, my eyes glinting with disgust.

"Scarlet, have you heard back from your intended collaborations?"

I bristled at his change of topic. I wasn't prepared to discuss this, but I wanted to sound confident—not like a pushover.

"We're waiting on an answer from both," I said. "Any day now, I'm sure."

"But are you in contact with them?"

"Well, Todd is keeping up with the business end, why do you ask?" I didn't want to admit that we hadn't heard back from Debauchee or that we were scheduled to meet with Caroline.

"Because I want you to think hard, Scarlet; figure it out. The clues are there," he said with a wink, despite his threatening tone.

"What clues? What are you talking about?"

This man was so cagey, I couldn't stand to be around him another minute.

He remained silent.

"Say something, please," I begged.

"All I can say is, be discreet and don't act carefree. Your science must be your first priority if you truly want to achieve your goals and act responsibly. If you won't agree to close Spells, then use your scientific mind and do it quickly. Time is of the essence. Find your passion in the darkness, not the light. Good luck."

He stood up and bid me farewell.

Each time I crossed paths with this man, I felt more and more ill at ease. It felt as though my heart was struggling to beat properly for the rest of the day. It took all my strength to lift myself out of the chair in the coffee shop and I plopped straight into bed when I arrived home. He could seriously qualify as a Dementor from the *Harry Potter* series.

Soon, the time came for our meeting with Caroline and Roseword. After my talk with Cole, I thought he would change his mind, but thankfully, he was still on board. He wanted to meet Caroline and Nikola, tour the factory, and see the injection machine he had heard so much about. I wasn't much for meddling, but I was glad he was joining us; he was such a successful businessman, and surely, he'd know what to say if an opportunity presented itself.

William even gave me a good luck charm before I left for the meeting: a golden egg. I promised him I'd keep it in my purse at all times, and I knew he would be watching over me.

Bright and early that morning, we walked into RICPCom's headquarters, and were greeted by Caroline and Nikola. It was nice to meet them in person after having e-mailed each other all this time. We walked into the large conference room and were offered tea and coffee, which we politely declined, before David, another researcher, who worked closely with Nikola, joined us.

"It's so nice to finally meet you," said Caroline.

"We couldn't be happier to be here," I said.

"Nikola tells me you have made serious progress since we last spoke, and that you have been keeping her updated," said Caroline.

I smiled and nodded; they looked pleased.

"We're here to present our latest results," said Todd, "and we really hope you'll like what you see."

Todd began the presentation, the same one that we had prepared for NavoLogic. I was looking for any hints or signs that they had already seen this presentation.

As Todd was talking about the motivations of automating the process and saving on incubation space and electricity and, of course, decreasing the manhandling of the newborn chicks, I interrupted.

"Caroline, may I ask you, were you here when they began to develop the injection machine?"

"Oh, yes," she said, smiling. "Those were exciting times, indeed. We have the prototype right outside."

"How did they sell it to the poultry corporations? What advantages did it have compared to manual vaccinations?" I asked.

"It wasn't so different from the advantages you are describing here," she said.

"Would you say they mainly bought it for the money they saved?" I asked.

"I think that is fair to say. If it had not saved them money, they probably would not have gone for it. That is why you need to make sure your product does not cost more than one-fifth of a cent per egg."

"By 'cost,' you mean what it will cost *us*, right?" Todd asked.

"Yes. I mean it should cost you no more than one-fifth of a cent and then your profit could be from one-tenth to three-tenths of a cent an egg. It depends on how it will fit in with our injection process and costs. Those are the numbers we came up with when we were working on our own method."

"*Were?*" I asked, surprised.

"Yes," she said with a frown. "Yes, we've given up on the research. We tested two other DNA methods, both of which worked perfectly, but one took four hours an egg, which was simply too long for multiple sampling, and the other was 95 percent accurate, but too expensive."

"You mentioned that it has to be done within fifteen minutes. Why is that?" asked Roseword.

"This is because if you want to reach the broiler industry, it is a huge number of eggs. If you do not process a tray within fifteen minutes, you will not have time to take them out and put them all back into the incubator in one day. The incubator is built like the inside of a spiral shell, so it takes time to just get all the eggs out and ready for injection. It's a lengthy and vulnerable process because each time you take them out of incubation, you risk the trays falling and eggs breaking. And, the more time they spend out of the incubator, the colder they get, and that affects the developing chick," answered Caroline.

"The good news is we can do it in less than one-fifth of a cent and within fifteen minutes," Todd said, gearing the talk back to the presentation. "We may be able to do it in less time, if Scarlet keeps up the great work."

David, Nikola's researcher, didn't seem like he believed it. Caroline asked Todd to go on with his presentation, and he did.

When he got to the animated graphic, David interrupted again: "You're saying your method works like a switch? So if it is female, the light is ON, and if it is male, the light is OFF, right?"

"Yes," I answered, growing impatient.

"But what happens if I am not seeing light because of another reason? Perhaps there is not enough of the extracted sample to test it? Can you verify that there is enough of the sample in the tube to be read?" he continued.

I tried to remember that you catch more flies with honey.

"That's a good question, David," I said, and saw Todd nodding approvingly. "Yes, I can. I have markers that output a different signal, which indicates how much sample is present and this is used as controls."

Todd passed quickly through the Cost Projections slide. I wanted to somehow convince them to take us under their wing. I wanted to be part of their team, even if they were far away. I wanted to be able to consult with other scientists regarding my work, to have someone with whom to go over the protocols and the experiments. I didn't want to work in a vacuum anymore.

Now it was Roseword's time to impress. He slickly pitched the notion of cleantech values, touting the financial gain that was to be made by marketing something with "green" technology.

"You can ask for more on that alone," he said. "Same with tuna cans and dolphin-safe labeling. Big poultry should pay a hefty amount to get this edge."

"Well, sir," she said, grinning, and I could tell the Roseword charm had worked on her, "I will certainly try to make that pitch to my superiors. It is an interesting idea."

"Public opinion can be very persuasive regarding these delicate matters," said Roseword, who then leaned back in his chair, looking like he had just said what he'd come to say.

Nikola was clearly impressed, but wanted to know if a prototype could be done within a year instead of our projected two. I balked, but admitted that if we got more brains and hands on deck, we could probably get it done.

"I agree," said Caroline, "if we put our heads together, we can do this, and fast. We'll need to get it out by next year."

After the presentation, Nikola proceeded to give us the tour of the facility. First, she showed us the prototype of the needle that proved that the eggs can be vaccinated. It was in a glass frame and engraved with the date at the bottom: *1991*. It didn't seem so long ago, I thought.

I realized why every time I talked with an elder veterinarian or farmer about my project, I could hear the excitement in their voice. They'd seen vaccination become automated firsthand. Their excitement had worn off on me and they'd led me to believe anything was possible; that we would indeed be able to sort chicks while they were still in the eggs. We wouldn't even have to stop at that; many more good things could become reality.

We walked on and saw the injection machine, which Roseword quickly approached. I could see the excitement in his eyes and I could tell he was imagining the same thing I was at that moment: that we could get this machine to extract a sample for sexing.

One of the technicians showed us how the machine worked, the various reading trays and the sizes. I was sad to hear that the development of Nikola's method had been stopped. I know she had put in a lot of work into it and had probably hoped, just as I had, that it would be successful. It isn't a good feeling when you don't get the results you want in science, but nature has its strict rules.

As we continued on the tour of the factory and facilities, Caroline walked beside me while the others followed behind us. She told me that she was very surprised by my having opened a company on my own, and my having the courage to believe in my own research. She said that when she was a young woman of my age, she was scared to death and could not have done what I was doing now.

"Do not get me wrong," I said, "I *am* scared to death!" We both laughed at that. They saw us to the door and we parted. Caroline said she'd be in touch after running things by management and the CEO, and that she hoped they could make us an offer within a few weeks.

chapter

26

We made plans to meet up with Caroline at a local park later in the day. For now, Roseword and I went to a local sandwich place and sat at a high-top table, looking out the window, happily watching the passersby.

"Do you think we should have asked them about Debauchee and NavoLogic?"

"Well, did Caroline mention she knew him when you talked to her last?" he asked.

"She was surprised to learn about the heartbeat method because she said she knew them well, but I don't know if she knows Debauchee personally."

"In any case, if she knows them well, she would have heard something about their plans," Roseword observed.

"I suppose you're right."

"I know what you're hinting at, Scarlet," he said.

We were quiet for a moment, the notion of how fragile our trust is in these people was hanging over us like a cloud.

"Do you really think someone wants to bury the project?" I asked him.

The expression on his face became grim.

After I had talked to William, I had reached out to Roseword to get him on the case; I knew it was old hat for him to hire private investigators for various business matters, and this would be easy enough for him to look into.

"I haven't found anything that leads to Caroline yet, Scarlet. But my men did find something."

I blanched.

"Your phone in your apartment was tampered with; it's been tapped."

The world started spinning. The joggers outside looked like they were blissfully unaware of everything—not just of me, but of every little implication of every horrible thing in the entire world. How badly I wanted to be on the other side of the glass window.

"What!?"

"You've definitely been compromised in some way at home. I didn't want to worry you, but I felt I had to tell you for your safety," he said.

"Well, gee, thanks," I said, becoming angry—but clearly, at the wrong person.

He didn't take it personally.

"There's one bright spot," he said. "The lab. They can't get you in there. Be thankful you rented a bench in a professional lab; otherwise, they would have gotten to you, no problem."

I told him about the time my sample had been contaminated.

"Could that have been their work?" I asked Roseword.

He nodded. "They could have persuaded someone from inside to do it. Or, more likely, whoever fills the equipment orders for the building."

"When did this start?"

"According to what they found, the phone tracking began shortly after your initial contact with RICPCom," he said. "But again, there's nothing that leads back to RICPCom."

"Who else could it be? Who is the snitch?" I asked.

He shrugged. "You've met a lot of people since you started this venture, Scarlet."

We talked more of what he knew, which wasn't much. He knew that everything appeared all clear at Todd's home, and I breathed a sigh of relief. Even though I didn't like the idea that someone was after *me*, at least I didn't have a family to protect. I thought of the golden egg in my purse, and thought that, at least, I had William and Roseword looking out for me.

"Do you think RICPCom will buy Spells?" I asked, braving a slight change of topic.

"I think they will," he said, nodding. "Especially if we help them strike a big deal with the pharma company. Your work shows a lot of promise, and they've done their due diligence. I think everyone will come away happy if they buy us now."

"Will I be able to pursue my other applications if they buy the chick-sexing solution?" I asked.

"It all depends how you patent it, how you sell it, and if you get further investments."

I was enjoying this private business-strategy class. My appetite had picked up again, and I even started to peck at my sandwich.

"But if I sell, I can invest that money in myself to do the other things I want to do, right?" I asked.

"You could potentially do that, but you really shouldn't invest in your own ideas. Kind of a no-no in the investment world," he said.

"Really?" I still had so much to learn.

"Really. You want to get others interested pretty quickly; you can't succeed in a vacuum like that," he said. "Furthermore, investors like crowds. They like to know everyone is putting down money on the same thing they are; it provides them with the reassurance they are looking for."

"But then if you win, you end up sharing the prize."

"I would rather share a prize than take all the risk upon myself. Some companies can go a long time without showing profit."

I shook my head. "I thought I saw something today," I said, slightly disappointed. "You seemed as excited about the ethics of the project as the monetary gains. Why bother to gamble, if not? Is it the thrill? You have everything you need already, and you will never want for anything."

"Rich people like to dream too, Scarlet," he said. "I need to be a part of something. That need didn't disappear when I became rich."

Later, Caroline and Todd joined us at the park, and we all strolled alongside a stream carpeted on both sides with beautiful green grass. I decided to tell Todd what was going on as soon as Roseword had figured out who had tapped my phone. But not now, there was no reason to break his reverie, since his privacy wasn't compromised.

chapter 27

had to be sure that nothing had been tampered with while we were gone. I called Roseword and asked him to meet me at the beachfront at the end of the day to talk, and then went straight to the lab to test my materials.

When I was in the lab, I smiled at everyone at work, as if my work there were just business as usual. I sat down and carefully checked my notebook. I set up a few tests to make sure the materials were good. I also ordered a cabinet that I could lock, so that I could then put everything in there and lock it each night before I left. I bought a cool blue 'Speed Dial™' lock for the fridge as well.

I kept working on my tests, but I was so tense that I kept pausing to look behind me. I thought I may have just developed a tic. My lab mates were there for most of the day, and I was grateful for their company; I felt like if I had been alone, I would have been in danger. Like someone would come out of the shadows and snuff me out. I'd never felt in danger before. I felt my smile freeze on my face while my thoughts were on fire, that absolute contrast. I constantly worried how fast I could cross back over to the safe side, to being me again. All I wanted to do was my usual worry-free research that I loved. I had never asked for this.

In the evening I headed over to the beachfront to meet with Roseword. We met on the sand, a naturally surveillance-free zone. The salt spray crashed against the shoreline, and I thought with a bit of wry humor that it was the perfect setting for the dramatic situation that my life had quickly become. I looked out at the roiling sea.

"Am I in danger?" I asked, remembering the paranoia that had engulfed me in the lab.

He shook his head. "I wish I could tell you one way or the other," he said. "I don't think so. I think this is more about the information than your personal safety. But for the sake of your sanity—and for the work—I think we should get someone to watch over the lab."

"Thanks," I said, laughing for the first time in a while. "You know, I'm still thinking about your offer to fly out of the country for cake. Maybe there, I'd feel safe."

"As long as I'm around, you can count on being safe."

I felt so grateful that we had him on our side. He leant new meaning to the term "angel investor." It was way more than he had signed up for.

In the following weeks, I stayed in the lab as much as possible, practically spending days and nights there. It was the only place I felt secure, now that I knew Roseword had the place watched by one of the good guys. But even though I was safe there, it was like I was locked into four walls through no fault of my own.

I brought a sleeping bag and slept in one of the small offices on the floor. At night, Cole's words would haunt me: "Find your passion in the darkness, not the light."

What did he mean by that? Words began to flash in my head. Why was I even thinking about this man?

And there was more going on. For weeks now I had been receiving what seemed like hidden messages in my e-mail: phishing. Advertisements popped up on my computer that correlated to things I'd texted about just minutes before. I knew that it had become a common practice, personalized advertising meant to follow your buying habits, but it felt creepy. Sometimes, I would notice patterns of words that just didn't belong in the context of the sentence, as if they were put there for me to find. Someone was sending me a code, but was it Cole? Was it real? Was it coincidental?

No, I thought. *His comments must have referred to my science. He must have just meant to say that I should concentrate on finding the secret sequence in order to solve the chicks' riddle and get the method finalized. But how would he know about the secret sequence I was searching for? Perhaps Roseword had confided in him?*

I wasn't sleeping well. I would wake up in the middle of the night, set up another reaction, turn on the machine, and go back to bed. Since a large part of doing molecular biology includes waiting for the incubation times, I could save a lot of time this way. I converted my stress into action.

One day, finally, a breakthrough: I found the sequence. I couldn't believe it when I saw it, and had to double-check several times. The amplification could truly be done! This meant that, most likely, I would not need to use Joel's method for amplification of the signal, and that my method would be self-sufficient! I stared at my result the whole night in my little "bedroom" in the small office on the floor, in my sleeping bag. I felt as if no one could possibly be happier than me in the whole wide world—not in the farthest corners or the biggest cities. Something positive had finally come out of what was becoming a stressful, potentially dangerous ordeal.

chapter 28

On the following Tuesday, I met with William and told him about the meeting with Caroline.

"I've got some news," he confided. "I'm doing some digging. I found out that next week, they're going to convene the board of directors at RICPCom to decide on your technology."

"Surprisingly, that's not news to me! Caroline told Roseword."

William shook his head. "That's not what the news is. Before that, they're scheduled to have a meeting with the pharma buyer. They've made an offer."

"What does that mean for us?"

"I read that they conditioned the price of the sale to rise if they bring in your technique. RICPCom is asking for more money if they include the chick sexing in the deal. If the pharma group says yes, they could make you an offer," said William.

"I hope so," I said.

He tilted his head and considered my expression.

"You seem a little down today, Scarlet."

"I'm a little tired," I admitted. "Some drama going on."

"Oh?"

"Yeah. Turns out you were right about the surveillance. I'm being followed."

He put his hand on top of mine gently.

"I'm so sorry. I hate that I was right about that."

"Me too," I said, and started to get up. "Anyway, I have to get going and get in bed early tonight. I have a meeting with Joel's investors tomorrow. He's made extensive progress. Even if we don't end up needing him for the chick sexing, he's excited about working together on other applications."

"That sounds interesting," he said.

"Yes, we prepared a whole new presentation for it. We even submitted papers for publication on it. He even has patents all set."

"Sounds like you have good friends," William said, and I appreciated the encouragement.

"Yeah, I have good friends, who certainly want good things for me, but sometimes a person needs a particular type of friend—one who helps in ways they can't even imagine. In a way, William," I said, and sighed, "I think you're that kind of friend. And I am so grateful for that."

He tried to act nonchalant and shrugged, but I saw a blush gathering in his cheeks. He looked down at his hands, and I continued my speech.

"Most of the time, people don't go out of their way to help others, or find excuses as to why they can't help. They just go about their business and worry about their own survival. You're not like that."

William cracked a smile, and I could tell he was going to try to take me off track.

"Should we get some chicken for dinner before you leave? I never asked if you were a vegetarian. I guess it makes sense that you might be," he said.

"I know it makes sense because I fight for animal rights in the food industry, but I am actually an omnivore," I admitted. "I used to be veggie for a couple of years, but now I think the fair solution is to lower my consumption of meat. I think the problem is that the industry lost that natural balance between predator and prey."

He seemed content to listen, so I continued. I wanted to let him in on more of me, on more of my philosophy.

"According to biologists, humans are carnivores, so we shouldn't apologize for wanting to eat meat; that's not the problem. Instead, the problem is the meat industry and its requirements. If people chose to eat less meat, the industry would have less reason to practice violent, inhumane practices."

"Interesting," he said. "So it's a matter of balance."

I nodded. He was getting me!

I went on: "I believe that chicken eggs are one of the most energy-rich natural resources we have, and that not consuming them is a shame. Eggs have got a really bad rap, but consider that no chick will develop from the eggs we eat; there is no sperm in them! So in that respect, it's not even meat. If it's about the cholesterol, then don't eat them every day. But not to consume them at all, as vegans choose to do? The female chicken goes through the energy-consuming process of producing them with or without us and they have all the required nutrients in them. Can we really afford that energy to be wasted? Isn't that hubris? If you see a soy field, would you choose to not eat from the soy because the farm workers put in energy and hard work to farm it, straining their bodies to do so?"

"I see your point, Scar, and I think you are right. Vegans have an issue with the industry probably more so than the food itself. It's the processing that needs to be regulated more humanely, and simply choosing to not eat it, won't make the problem go away because there will always be enough people who will eat it, and *lots* of it."

"So to answer your question William, thank you, I would love to eat some chicken before I head home, because if I eat any more pie today, I will break the cross-trainer the minute I get on it."

"Great!" he signaled to the waiter to put in an order and added some pie too, just to be on the safe side.

"If I didn't know better, I would think you are trying to fatten me up and then roast me."

"I look beyond the obvious Scar, a person's character is worth more than flashiness and glitter. Besides, I like my women big and beautiful, so eat up. I like a woman who appreciates the simple things in life, like eating; then I know she will be dreaming about food instead of other men."

"Very funny," I said.

chapter 29

I was knee-deep in a daydream about what it would be like when this mess was all over, when Todd came into the lab, clearly excited.

"I got a phone call from Debauchee!" he exclaimed. "He wants to meet with us in person. In France."

I smiled from ear to ear.

"How exciting is that? I was wondering why he was being so shy about committing when he'd said they had three projects they were looking for. What about Caroline, though? Shouldn't we postpone until we get a reply from her, one way or the other?" I asked Todd.

"Definitely not! We need to take every opportunity we get. This is business, and in business, you take every opportunity."

"What will we show them? We already went over our presentation on the conference call."

"They want to get into more detail. Who knows, perhaps they'll ask us for a demonstration."

I hesitated. "I do have a draft I've been writing together with Professor Frolev. We're hoping to publish on the work," I said.

"Publishing is always good for business. But are you ready to show it?" Todd asked.

"I think it could be ready. I'll ask Frolow."

"Sounds like a plan. I'll work on preparing any necessary nondisclosure forms," he said.

I rolled my eyes. "I'm more than happy to let you handle that."

A few days later, everything was ready for the meeting. Todd had scheduled the flights, bought the tickets, and even booked a taxi to take us to the airport. It was a relief to be getting out of town for a while, away from the bogeymen, who may or may not be following my every move. I was packing the final few items in my suitcase when I got a call from a breathless Roseword. I knew something was wrong as soon as I picked up the phone; I'd never heard him sound anything but completely confident before.

"Scarlet, drop what you're doing and meet me at the hospital," he said.

My heart clenched up and rose into my throat. What could it be?

"Something happened to Joel," he said. "Meet me in the emergency room."

When Todd and I got there, Roseword was sitting in the waiting room. He pointed to a closed door and said that Joel was in there with an ophthalmologist.

"What happened?"

"I'm not sure," Roseword said, shaking his head. "We had a meeting scheduled today at Joel's lab. When I got there, he was writhing on the floor screaming, holding his hands over his eyes, saying that he'd been burned by a laser from one of his machines."

My heart sank. That kind of equipment is powerful stuff; I had no doubt that Joel had been blinded. And he was too much of an expert to be fooling around with the equipment, so that meant it probably had been tampered with.

"Did anyone check out the machine?" I asked.

"One of his lab mates just called to confirm that the laser had been repositioned," said Roseword. "It doesn't seem to be accidental, unfortunately."

I kept thinking about what William had said, about our safety, particularly Joel's. But how could I have known exactly how this would happen, and when? How could I have prevented it? And how had William known? What was going on?

I was praying for Joel to be all right. I felt that I might die if I heard he'd become permanently blind—his whole career, gone. I tried to choke back my tears, but they began to fall. I told Todd through sobs that we needed to call NavoLogic and tell them we couldn't make it there on time, that we'd had an emergency.

We waited, and it felt like an eternity. Then the doctor came out and said, much to our relief, that he felt optimistic that Joel would regain sight. He said that ocular flashes might remain, and that it was too soon to tell the extent of the damage, but it seemed as if this might have been a warning shot more than anything else.

With that, the doctor left us, saying that we could go in and see Joel. We slowly trod into the room, dreading what we were going to see. Even though the damage might not be permanent, it was still heartbreaking to think of Joel in this position. All he was trying to do was the work we had asked him to do, and here we were.

Joel was sitting on the bed, drinking from a straw. Occasionally, he'd lose track of the straw and would have to go groping for it with one hand.

"How are you feeling?" I asked. "Can you see us? Anything?"

"I can sort of see you," he said with a grimace. "It's all fuzzy. And black-and-white. The doc thinks I'll be OK. We just have to run a few more tests and see what happens."

"We heard," I said, taking his hand. "Are you in any pain?" I took a chocolate bar out of my purse, the kind he said was his favorite, and pressed it into his other hand.

"No, they gave me painkillers, so my eyes feel better," he said. "They were burning before, though. It felt like explosions were going off in my skull."

We sat quietly for a moment, mostly staring at the floor. We weren't sure how much eye contact to make with Joel. How much could he see? Thankfully, he closed his eyes and leaned back against his pillow, breathing deeply and trying to calm down. His adrenaline must have been pumping like crazy.

"I hate to ask you this, Joel," started Roseword, "but is there *any* chance at all that you could have moved the laser by accident?"

Joel shook his head. "None. None whatsoever."

"That's what I was afraid of," said Roseword, before telling us that he was going to leave to check the security logs with his watchmen.

"Maybe it could have been someone you share the space with," I suggested.

"I really don't think so, Scarlet," said Joel.

I nodded. I had gone through all the same worries and machinations when my lab had been tampered with. I hadn't wanted to accept the truth, but it seemed that Joel was more ready to do so.

To my surprise, Todd broke in with what I felt was a horribly inappropriate question.

"Joel," he said, "do you mind terribly if we took a flight out today? We have a meeting with NavoLogic in France."

It took all my restraint not to elbow him in the ribs.

"We can't leave him alone like this!" I exclaimed.

Joel shook his head. "Scarlet, don't be silly. You *have* to go. If anything happens, I'll give you a call. And I've got our angel, Roseword."

We said our good-byes, each giving Joel a big hug, and left for the airport in a hurry.

hoped that Joel would, indeed, be in good hands. Luckily, we had insurance that would pay for the best treatment—whatever he needed. I thought of William again. How could he have known?

On the flight to Paris, I asked Todd about the logistics of getting to the company headquarters in Nancy. I smiled, thinking to myself that I'd always liked the name *Nancy.*

"We'll take the TGV high-speed train. Their manufacturing plant is just outside Nancy, actually, although we'll be staying there," Todd answered.

"I heard that Nancy is a wonderful place," I said, thinking about the quick daydreaming I was able to do once we found out we'd be going to see the NavoLogic execs in person.

"I think anywhere you go in France is beautiful," said Todd. "And let's not even start talking about the food! There is nothing like it in the world."

"I can't wait," I said, and then started to feel guilty about my excitement. I closed my eyes and tried to relax after the crazy morning we'd had. Todd wanted to talk and make plans, of course, and I entertained him for a little while, but while he was talking, I couldn't help but doze off. I was exhausted.

The trip was not meant to go off without a hitch, it turned out. If the day had started out the way it had, something else was bound to go wrong, and, indeed, when we got off the plane, we found out that my luggage had been lost. By the time we had made the arrangements at the lost-luggage counter, the last TGV train had left for the night. The men at the counter told us we would need to come pick up the luggage tomorrow morning, and so we would have to remain in Paris for the night.

Todd could tell I was crestfallen, but he told me not to worry. Todd, ever the world business traveler, knew an inexpensive hotel where he had stayed a few times before. We took a cab to a place by Paris-Gare de Lyon and knocked loudly to wake up the hotel keeper. The sign read, *No entry after midnight,* but we were still hoping to get in. After all the commotion we'd made, a middle-aged man came out with nightcaps— the hat and the drink, both. Todd managed to explain to him in halting French that if he had two rooms available, we would really appreciate it. He explained that we had come from afar.

The man said he only had one vacant room, and as if to underscore the point, drunkenly waggled a single finger in our faces. What were we going to do: search for another hotel? I tried to explain that we weren't a couple, but the hotel keeper just kept shaking his head, finally saying in heavily accented English: "One room or no room." So, we took it.

We climbed up five flights of rickety stairs until we reached the room, there being no elevator in sight. Just then, I was somewhat relieved that I did not have my suitcase with me. The room was small with a double bed and bathroom with a toilet, a bidet, and a tiny closet. There was a nice, big window, but in the dark, there was no view to be enjoyed.

Todd was kind enough to offer to sleep on the floor. Even though we had absolutely no romantic feelings toward one another, we'd never shared a space before, and being in the same hotel room with him, in a strange city, with his kids thousands of miles away, it felt awkward. He was also kind enough to let me use an extra pair of shorts and a shirt he brought, and he slept shirtless. Luckily, it was summer, and he would be warm enough even with a window open to allow in a breeze.

I lay awake in bed for a couple of hours, unable to sleep. Apparently, I wasn't alone in the predicament. At one point, after a long silence, he asked me why I didn't have kids yet. It was then apparent to me that he missed his family, and it made me feel more comfortable. It was a question he'd never asked me before. I answered simply that I wanted to be a mother one day, but I was waiting for that special feeling to come to me. In the meantime, I had so much I wanted to accomplish.

Now I felt free to ask him why he had four. He replied that it was mainly his wife's decision, but that once they'd had this big family, everything had come together and made him feel whole. He said that if he were to reconsider it again today, he would choose to have four kids and not one fewer.

Todd and I spent half the night talking, as if it were a slumber party. He told me about his kids and I told him about myself and my past relationships. I explained that I was waiting for a man who would love me and ask me to be the mother of his children before I cried from happiness, and not after I had cried from sadness. Many of the young women I'd met who had begged and pleaded to get a commitment from the men they had chosen had cried from sadness.

"That's probably why you don't have kids yet, Scarlet," he said. "Nobody's good enough for you! And I mean that as a compliment."

We finally fell asleep just as the first light of dawn was trickling through the window. Some time later, I woke up to the sound of Todd's smartphone ringing; it was nearly noon, and we had to rush back to the airport to check on my suitcase. But more important, we needed to let the NavoLogic folks know that we wouldn't be making the two o'clock meeting due to our delay.

Todd called Debauchee and apologized for ten minutes, spinning a story about travel woes. After his lengthy apology, Debauchee seemed all right with the delay. He was very generous, and even said they would send a car out to Paris with a driver to pick us up from the airport after we retrieved my suitcase.

We set out to the airport, passing by a few empty rooms with doors half open as the cleaning ladies worked inside. We passed by the hotel keeper, and he had a grin on his face. He greeted us with a good afternoon and asked Todd how the *one* room worked out for us. I put on an even bigger grin and looked at Todd lovingly. I put my head on his shoulder and we both just stared at the hotel keeper. He was full of himself and happy that he had "taught" us the French way of romance.

chapter

31

When we got to the airport another disappointment was waiting for us: my suitcase was nowhere to be found. Todd and I were not going to let this spoil our day. I told him that, after all, we were in Paris and we should be able to find a nice suit for me to wear. We called the driver and asked him to meet us five hours later at a corner café near the Champs-Élysées. A half a day in Paris can do wonders for anyone, especially me. To be out in that beautiful city with the sun shining in the sky was a precious experience. I started to think about William, and how it would feel to have him here with me.

Todd, who had been to the city before, took me to the best clothes boutiques we could find, waiting patiently as I tried on a few things.

"Why don't you try a dress instead of a suit, Scarlet?" he said.

He suggested a flowery spring dress with sunflowers, and a flowery perfume to go with it. I had no problem at all choosing a joyful fragrance. Buying perfumes was one of my favorite indulgences, and I liked the French fragrances the most. Nothing like a classic Chanel to make my spirits rise. I bought the dress, and he approved. I knew I would not be caught dead in a dress like this one back home; I was more of a lab-coat-and-jeans kind of gal. Still, when I put on this dress and stepped into the summer sun in Paris, I felt like I was walking on air.

I asked Todd if he needed a new suit.

"If I walk in with this pretty dress," I said, giving a little spin, "you might need a new suit to match it!"

I was happy for the rare chance to shop. We went suit searching, and wrapped up our time in Paris by buying three perfumes, one of which I had promised to give as a gift. He bought two bottles of men's cologne and a perfume for his wife, as well as some small perfume gift sets. Todd's were for his children, and mine was a gift to myself.

When we got into the cab sent by Debauchee, we smelled as colorful as we possibly could, and the driver drove us out to Nancy. The drive took a few hours, and we were sorry it was too late to enjoy the view once the sun had set. The driver brought us to an exquisite hotel and told us it was on the house. NavoLogic was sorry about our delays, and wanted to make us feel at home. They made sure to give us two rooms, and I knew we'd be sleeping in more comfortable quarters tonight. The driver said he would come by the next morning to pick us up and take us to the factory, which was about an hour's drive away. We thanked him and checked in. Todd loaned me the shorts and shirt to sleep in again, and then we said good night, each retiring to our own room for a good night's sleep.

When we stepped out into the cab the next morning, I was in my new dress, and Todd, in his new suit, and we were both ready for a very important meeting. Dubreuil and Debauchee greeted us as we pulled up to the entrance of a huge manufacturing building. It was exciting, to say the least. You could feel the energy in the air.

We walked into a small conference room and sat down around a table that I recognized from our video conference—virtual reality, come to life. They wasted no time getting started.

"Scarlet, our scientific advisory board read the information you sent, and they were very impressed," said Debauchee. "We are interested in getting more details from you to understand how you are going to approach the project if you join our group."

I looked at Todd before I replied and he nodded, giving me the go-ahead. I pulled out the draft of the paper that Professor Frolev and I intended to submit for publication.

"Thank you, gentlemen," I said, and nodded at each of the French executives. "I brought copies of a paper with me that describes the method we're developing. I think it'll give you the answers you're looking for."

I passed out the copies to each of the men.

"Let's begin by understanding the technical problems we are trying to overcome. As we already know, the aim of the project is to segregate the chicks before they hatch, of course. The plan is to segregate the eggs in the trays while they are on the conveyer belt waiting to get vaccinated. It should take no more than fifteen minutes per tray to get the results. So the method we are describing here aims to lay the groundwork for achieving this goal. I'll describe the method, but let me just say that it would be optimal if I had a way to show you the process in the lab," I said.

"Would you like us to set up a bench for you so that you can show us?" asked Dubreuil.

"I would love that. Technically, we have shown that it can be done in fifteen minutes, but it all has to be assembled to work on the conveyer belt and that challenge will take some more research and development," I answered.

"Fair enough. I think we can organize a lab for you," said Debauchee, and Dubreuil nodded in agreement. "Let's continue."

"So, as you can see in this draft of the research, the chicks can be sexed *in ovo* within fifteen minutes. We tested the method at different incubation times," I said, pointing to the biological results.

"Another part of the assembly that we need to work on is the sample extracted from the egg. Until now, we have used blood, but we would like to examine the amniotic and allantoic fluids thoroughly to see if they can be used instead. Ideally, we would like to have a lab injection machine to use for our research. This will allow us to test different samples from the egg directly in the same way they would be extracted by the injection machine in the incubators. Currently, I extract a sample manually and the samples vary. If I had the machine, I could gather real statistical information about the DNA content of the sample."

"I see," said Debauchee. "And once you decide on the best sample to use, you will have overcome all your obstacles?"

"The sample should contain enough DNA for me to be able to achieve results with my method. So far, I have shown that it does, but I need to gather more statistical information, specifically using the injection machine we'll be using in the end product," I answered as best and honestly as I could. "There's still work to be done; we're not completely there yet."

"We will surely understand more once we see what you have done in the lab," said Debauchee.

We continued our discussion in further detail before breaking for lunch, hungry and happy to take them up on their offer for some delicious local fare. They promised that after lunch, we'd get a full tour of the facility, which I was very much looking forward to.

They took us to lunch at a rather fancy French restaurant, which amused me because by my estimation, French food can never be bad. If you took me to both a cheap French place and a fancy French place, I would find the food at each a hundred times better than what I eat every day.

The food did not disappoint. It was a fabulous four-course meal with a pastry appetizer, chicken cordon bleu, strawberry sorbet made from real strawberries and no added sugar, followed by a cheese plate. To die for. I thought that if I had to relocate to France to work, I wouldn't get much done, because I would spend all my time eating, and then they would have to ship me back home.

Lunch wasn't used for talking science or business, mainly because I had my mouth full of food the entire time. While I ate ravenously, Todd told the two men a little about how we met and started Spells, in addition to the story of who had joined us along the way.

Later that afternoon on the tour, we got to see the different equipment NavoLogic manufactures. Oddly enough, it reminded me of Joel's workspace. I was dismayed to see that there were only men working in the facility, not a woman in sight. *I would change that,* I thought.

I got a few whistles as I strolled down the factory floor in my flowery dress, careful to ignore the attention. Debauchee and Dubreuil scowled at the perpetrators. They showed us their offices and a couple of big conference rooms too. I excused myself to the restroom as soon as we passed by one and Todd did the same. I immediately called him on his cell phone so we could quickly and stealthily discuss the meeting we'd just had. I then called Joel and asked him how he was feeling. He was doing better, relaxing at home, and he was happy for us that the meeting had seemed to go well.

The NavoLogic executives said they would organize for us to visit a research lab the next day and that we could then talk about what we would need for showing our lab experiments. It would take a couple of weeks to order and get everything set up, so we discussed the option of us flying back once again for this, and agreed it would be a possibility if we were to move forward.

We said our good-byes and left, reassured by Debauchee that we would meet again very soon. We agreed that we would send them all the written information we had concerning what we'd discussed and they agreed to sign our nondisclosure agreement. We shook on it and left, my dress flying up in the slight wind.

The driver drove us to the nearby town of Metz while we rested in the backseat on the way there. Once we arrived in Metz, we saw amazing churches and gardens that gave it its apt nickname: "The Green City." We passed by a small café and asked the driver to stop so we could get some coffee. He let us off and said he would be back in an hour. We stopped at a *crêperie* and ate chocolate crêpes and then proceeded to the coffee shop. I was floating on air.

"I think that went well. What about you?" I asked Todd, optimistic and my mouth full of chocolate.

"It is exciting! They seemed very interested. We will see what develops tomorrow."

The next morning, we were taken to a lab at the local university. The professor there, Dr. Holland, introduced himself and welcomed us. He asked his student, Sandrine, to show us around his lab and to introduce us to the others. While walking around, I checked out their equipment. I found it to be standard lab equipment, and the rooms were spacious and the benches, clean. It seemed they lacked for nothing.

We went into a room filled with chemicals and I asked the Ph.D. student where they kept a certain chemical. She replied simply, in French, that she didn't know. I thought that was a bit strange, since this was a very basic chemical used to prepare standard buffers. When I asked her how she prepares the buffers, she answered that the professor brings the chemicals to the bench and then they can prepare what they need. She said they couldn't go into this room alone to take whatever they want.

As we walked through the building and she mentioned other things they couldn't touch without the professor's supervision, I found it to be a bit restrictive. This process would mean that each student scientist was constantly dependent on the professor in order to get anything done. Back in my Masters Degree in Science days, if I would've dared to ask my professor to retrieve a basic chemical for me out of the closet, he would have kicked me out faster than I could say the name of that chemical. Independence was the essence of my university training. I would have to make sure this was not common practice, because if it was, and I ended up coming here, I wouldn't fit in well at all. Especially since I prefer to work after hours.

Suddenly, a female student came up to us and asked Todd if he could help them lift open the centrifuge lid. Five petite women were standing around a huge centrifuge, helplessly waiting for a man to come and help them push up the lid. I walked over with Todd, put my hand across his chest and stepped forward to do it myself. The student tried to stop me, explaining it would be too hard, that it was a man's job. I had four centrifuges, exactly the same, in my lab at home and I knew very well how to push them open. They just stared at me as I did it, shocked, and I walked away. I'd never let a man do that job for me.

After the centrifuge incident, we sat down in Dr. Holland's office, where we were met by Dubreuil and Debauchee. I gave a short summary to Holland and wrote down a list of the things I would need in order to perform my experiment. We went over the expenses, which were then approved by Dubreuil.

Debauchee then made up some excuse to take me into a separate room of the lab, saying that he wanted me to check out a certain piece of machinery. I felt that this was odd, but followed him anyway. Once we were alone, he took me aside and whispered quickly that he had received a phone call and that someone was threatening him to avoid doing business with us. He explained that this was the sole reason he could not make us an offer yet, and he had been waiting to catch me alone to confide in me.

I just stood there in shock, frozen. This was a complete surprise. By the look on my face, he understood immediately that I had no idea whom the culprit could be. Just then, we were interrupted by Dubreuil, who came in to tell us that the tour should finish up in the cafeteria.

The food looked positively gourmet, but I didn't have much of an appetite after what I'd just heard.

Our business done, our journey at a close, we took our seats on the plane, and Todd immediately fell asleep. I, on the other hand, was still shaken up after that short talk I'd had with Debauchee. Now it was clear to me why he'd asked us to come to France to meet him face-to-face. He had wanted to figure out for himself if there was something serious going on, and if we were in on it, or if we were as in the dark as he was.

Angrily, I thought of the guilty party, the mystery voice on the other end of the phone. Why would someone be so cruel as to undermine the legitimacy of our research? And what would happen with NavoLogic now? Would this threat turn them against investing in us, or would it accomplish exactly the opposite?

My thoughts started to spiral into paranoia, as they often did after I'd heard that my phone had been bugged. I needed to talk to Roseword as soon as we landed. Were they responsible for my lost suitcase? Could it be? Was that meant to deter me from getting to the meeting? Or were they trying to get information that they thought I'd packed in my suitcase? The secret sequence, possibly? Or was I imagining it, and this was a casual airport mistake?

I desperately needed to find who was behind all these tricks: having me followed, messing with my lab materials, threating Debauchee, and Joel's accident! I had to talk to William; I knew he would reassure me and make me feel better. I looked forward to his hug so much.

chapter 32

As soon as we'd safely landed, I pulled out my phone and called Joel. "How are you?" I asked, my heart beating hard. I hoped he was on the mend.

"I'm fine, thanks," he said, and I was relieved, because he sounded good. "I go back to work in a couple of days."

I asked if he thought he might be feeling up to going to the little café by our farm. I was stopping by there to pick up some eggs, and it would make me happy to be able to take him to lunch. He agreed, and we met there, out in the sunshine. Joel was wearing dark eyeglasses for protection, but otherwise, he seemed well. Todd and Roseword had joined us so that we could all talk about what had transpired in France. It was a joyful day, all in all, the meeting ending with Roseword clapping us on the backs and saying that he'd be happy to live in France for a couple years if he had to do so.

"You really know how to take one for the team," I said.

As tired as I was that night, I knew I had to make my way to the pub to see William. It was Tuesday, the night of our weekly meeting. When I came in and he got up to walk toward me, I leapt into his arms and gave him a big hug.

"I have excellent news," I whispered in his ear as he took my hand and led me to our usual table.

"I'm guessing the meeting went well in France?" he asked.

"Boy, did it ever! We had a wonderful meeting, and they're even giving us a time slot in a lab to show them our method," I said, a huge smile on my face.

He gave me a stone-faced look, like he was going to remain in business mode.

"I want to see all the data," he said, before finally cracking a smirk.

"France was unbelievable."

"I can tell. What a dress!" he said, eyeing my bright, new number.

I blushed. "I decided I had to wear it tonight to see if it worked for me at home, or if it only worked in France."

"Is this what you wore for the meeting?" he asked with utter surprise. I guess he knew I wasn't a dress person. "Unbelievable!"

"What is unbelievable is that they liked us! And the more they heard, the more engaged they became. I got a good feeling from them, and I really believe they can help us get this project going."

"They want you?" he teased.

"Yes, why not?"

"Well, of course, in that dress, who wouldn't?"

"They want me for my *mind*, William."

"Uh-huh."

"Stop! it's true! They think I have good ideas."

"Well, you will set them straight soon enough," he said with a smile. I liked the banter we had going; it made me feel like the connection between us was real and mutual.

"I loved their food."

"You love food, period."

"I know, I know; I am a foodie," I admitted, "but this food! It was . . . *indescribable."*

"I'll take your word for it. Does it mean you don't want our plain little pie tonight?"

"Well, I do. But before I eat the pie, I should make sure it is not poisoned," I said, cloaking truth in jest. My mind had turned to the warning he'd given me about Joel.

"Why?"

"Tell me how you knew Joel was going to get hurt," I said.

"Joel was hurt? What happened to him?" He seemed genuinely surprised, even though he had been the one to give me the warning.

I told William about the dramatic morning of our flight—the laser beam, the emergency room, all of it. He became quiet and serious.

"I'm really not playing around, William," I said. "I need to know."

He put up his hands in a gesture to indicate that he couldn't reveal his sources.

"I hope that expensive insurance you got him helped, at least?"

I stopped, my blood running cold. I was sure I hadn't told him about that. I ate my pie and stole suspicious glances at him. He was strange, that was for sure. But I had a good instinct about him. Something told me he was one of the good guys.

chapter 33

The summer ground down to an eerily dead halt. I didn't even see William on our usual nights. After a long period of waiting for something—anything—to happen, finally, some good news arrived. Caroline at RICPCom had called Roseword and shared that they'd been sold to Flink Pharmaceuticals for the price of $200 million. Soon, she'd said, RICPCom and Flink would probably be able to make a deal with us, and everything would fall into place. She had even asked Roseword to join her at the next Flink board meeting, and had booked him a flight out later that night.

When he called to tell me of his travel plans, I insisted that we meet before he left. I knew I had to tell him about my conversation with Debauchee, as well as the fact that he had disappeared and we hadn't heard from him since. Todd couldn't get ahold of him; all of his attempts came up dry.

We agreed to meet at the beachfront that evening before his flight. I liked to stand in the sand, where I felt safe, like no one was listening. While I waited for him to arrive, I took my shoes off and let my toes sink into the warm sand. I loved that feeling. But despite the comfort of that familiar sensation, the more I thought about Debauchee's warning, the more distraught I became. Everything had been just about to start, and it seemed so promising. Why was this happening? Why were we in danger?

When Roseword showed up and I told him what had happened, he didn't seem surprised.

"Well, that fits with what we know so far. Someone isn't happy with your work," he said. "We should lie low. Tell you what, Scarlet, let's not attempt to contact NavoLogic, and instead, we'll wait and see if they contact you. Go on about your business as usual in the lab."

I felt like if I had to go through another day of waiting, I would spontaneously combust. I had barely made it through those last few weeks.

"This is becoming a nightmare," I said. "How can I wait? We said we would arrange a time to come back there and show them our method in the lab. They must have already ordered the materials."

"Then wait for them to contact you regarding the lab test. He didn't tell you the exact nature of the threat, correct?" he asked.

"No, but he explained that it was the reason he had not yet made us an offer," I said. "He doesn't want this public."

"Do not worry Scarlet. This is not your fault," said Roseword. "The only thing we can do is continue working on our project. We have an important goal to reach."

Roseword advised me to be very careful, both about my personal security and the security of my materials in the lab. He said he would make a few phone calls to try to get to the bottom of all this, and reassured me that as long as I was not being directly threatened, we should continue the project as planned.

Before he left for his meeting with Caroline, I wished him luck. Then, to calm down, I went for a run in the sand. *What could this mean? What should we do?* I knew I needed to speak to William, but first, I had to make an important call.

I contacted my initial source at NavoLogic, who had originally given me information about the heartbeat method. He didn't know about anything suspicious, but he did confirm that Debauchee was adamant about forging a connection with Spells.

I asked him about the progress of the heartbeat method and he said they were progressing, but that they'd had difficulties with getting the error ratio down; however, they hadn't given up.

Following that call, I went directly to the pub and made a beeline for the corner table. Thankfully, for the first time in weeks, William was sitting there. I missed him so.

"You're not going to believe what happened," I said, frowning.

"You missed me?"

I was in no mood for banter, no matter how handsome he looked.

"I had really good news to share, but now I have really bad news too."

"Start with the good news," he said.

"The good news is that we got an e-mail from Debauchee's secretary at NavoLogic. She said our data and results had passed the scientific advisory board's approval and they were just waiting on final confirmation from management."

"That is great news!" he smiled and got up to give me a hug, but I sat him back down again before he could do that. I needed to tell him the bad news.

"Right, but . . ."

"Debauchee is missing," he finished—his brow, furrowed.

"This isn't funny anymore, William. Who are your sources?" I felt myself becoming agitated. "I need to know what's going on. Are you really even my friend?"

He looked sad and winded, like he'd been punched in the gut. I felt pained that I had hurt him, but my world was in disarray. I had to know what was going on.

He reached across the table and took my hands.

"Listen carefully," he said. "You really need to be careful with this project. RICPCom is desperate for your solution, and they know you've been going behind their back to competitors. They also know about the heartbeat method, and they don't want that to fly. They are wrapping up the pharma sale, and they can't take any risks. Do you know what I'm saying?"

I gulped and nodded. If we didn't go with RICPCom, something bad might happen . . . in addition to the bad things that had already happened, of course.

"Are you saying Debauchee's disappearance has something to do with my method?"

"Exactly," said William, his expression, grim.

"And how do you know all this?"

He shook his head. "I'll tell you some other time. But right now, you need to get in touch with RICPCom and tell them you want to meet. Don't mention Debauchee or NavoLogic. Take Todd and fly out there for a meeting. Give them the impression that you're in the palm of their hands."

I felt nauseous suddenly, and very, very tired. We talked for a while longer, hashing out a plan for me to finish my research as quickly as I possibly could—and, of course, without letting anyone know my findings. I'd need to play my cards close to my chest. I let out a sigh and asked William to walk me home.

"Certainly," he agreed. "And don't forget to call Roseword and clue him in on this as well. Just don't do it over the phone. You can trust him, but your phone may be bugged."

But Roseword is already on his way to Caroline, I thought. I felt like I was about to cry.

"I just wanted to sort chicks, not develop nuclear arms, William," I said. "What is going on?"

"Scarlet, you're talking about a billion-dollar industry owned by a few, powerful people who like things to go their way," he said, shaking his head. "But you just keep your head down. Do what you're good at. Keep on with the science."

We walked home quietly in the dark, and at one point, I felt myself leaning into William a bit as we walked.

"I feel like you're protecting me, but what are *you* getting out of it?" I asked. "Don't *you* need a listening ear, a shoulder to lean on?"

I wondered why he hadn't ever offered me any of his contact information. I guessed that he might not be ready for any type of commitment, and I'd have to settle for these meetings over pie and beer. But no matter what was going on in my life, I felt the desire to hold him close, to keep him safe.

chapter 34

worked hard, memorizing my results, keeping the secret sequence I'd sought and discovered locked in my head and nowhere else. We continued to hear nothing from NavoLogic, and Debauchee remained off the radar.

As I worked in the lab, I couldn't help but feel totally alone, completely down. I had always been the type of person to offer all the help I possibly could; anyone who had worked with me could attest to that. But now, when I felt like I needed help, who would be there for me?

When Cole walked through the door, I felt my face fall; he wasn't the solution I had been hoping for. *And what's with dropping by unannounced? Can't the man send an e-mail?* I wondered. I was annoyed.

I tried to smile politely.

"Welcome to my humble establishment."

"Did I not explain to you what you should and shouldn't be doing? Have you read my e-mail messages?"

"Sorry, no, they must have slipped into my spam folder. I didn't realize that when Roseword put his own money on me, it required me to report to you."

"I am his right-hand man, no matter where the money comes from. You would be wise to listen to reason. I asked you to not to pursue this, right? Where is Roseword now?"

"You're his right-hand man, after all. Don't *you* know where he is?"

"I told you things would go wrong if you cross me," he said in a quiet but firm voice.

"Roseword is with Caroline now. I wasn't aware I was crossing you. I have always tried to be polite to you and have taken seriously the clues you mentioned."

"Have you found it?"

"Found what?"

"Don't mess around here!" he demanded.

"The solution?" I asked hesitantly, fishing for answers, myself.

"Yes!" he replied, his eyes widening. He didn't move a muscle, like a tiger stalking his prey.

I felt the hair on the back of my neck stand up. I realized I was all alone in the lab. When my phone rang, I jumped.

"Roseword, hi! We were just talking about you. Cole is here; he was asking about where you are. Would you like to talk to him?"

I handed Cole the phone and walked slowly to push the red call button that Roseword had set up for me in case I ever had an emergency.

Cole finished his conversation with Roseword, hung up, and handed me the phone. He walked over to the door, saying something about how he was in a hurry. As he was leaving, a security man walked in. I signaled to him that everything was fine and he walked Cole outside the building. I breathed a sigh of relief.

I sat down on my bench, the most comforting place in the world, and continued working. In a way, I felt ungrateful, feeling so fatalistic. We were expecting a positive answer from Caroline and RICPCom, and it seemed there was hope. But underneath, it felt like rocks were tumbling onto smooth stones in my stomach. I felt as though the world as I knew it was crumbling around me.

I had started to doubt everything. I needed to talk to William. He was the only one who could make me feel better, but I could only see him on Tuesday, and it was a Friday. *How ridiculous is that? How much more pathetic can I be? Waiting for a guy who will not give me his number? Waiting to hear from a professional who liked my ideas and then disappeared? Waiting for my investor to work his business magic? Waiting for Nikola to set aside her bruised ego and endorse me? Waiting for Caroline to promote a younger woman? Begging the people who live in the forest with nothing to eat, to take my healthy newborn chicks that I could not take back to the farm?* I asked myself, doubting my purpose. *Would the chicks really feel less pain, if we achieved sexing in ten days instead of twenty-one, when they hatch? When do they begin feeling pain?*

Roseword's meeting with Caroline was delayed—first, by days, and then, by weeks. With everything going on with the Flink Pharmaceuticals acquisition, it was no surprise. He called often to let us know that resolution would come soon enough. I tried to be as patient as I could, though it was hard to keep my spirits up after I had begun to sink into the doldrums.

Then, it happened. The big day. Roseword came back into town and suddenly appeared at my door in the lab. I was shocked. When I saw his face, I could tell it wasn't good news, and my heart started splinter into a thousand tiny pieces.

"Please, I can't handle any more bad news," I said.

"We need to talk," he said, looking around. "In private." I had never seen him so down before.

"No one died, right?" I asked, and we started walking. I was relieved when he shook his head. I felt like I couldn't take that kind of thing for granted anymore.

He looked at the ground as we walked along, saying nothing for a long time, and then finally: "I gave it my best shot, Scarlet. I swear."

"How many of them were there?"

"About twelve on the board."

"And only one of you," I said. "I'm so sorry you had to go in there alone."

"Caroline was there for me—and she was totally on our side," he said.

Some part of me was pleased to hear that; I wanted to know who to trust.

"Why did they say no in the end?"

"Who knows why? They gave some excuse, said they were just in the process of being sold and transferred, and that establishing the research and development would take time, and that they were discontinuing their chick-sorting research," he replied.

"But were there also representatives from Flink?"

"Yeah. They sang the same song. Process, time, not sure where they're going, all that nonsense."

"What about the edge that chick sexing would bring?"

"Caroline had already made the case. They had seemed to accept it earlier, but now, they've done a total 180. No explanation, nothing to go on," he said. "I'm so sorry."

That was the final straw, I burst into tears.

He put his arm on my shoulder.

"Not you, too! Caroline cried all last night."

"All that buildup? All the expectation? And no reason for this change of heart?"

"None. They complimented your idea. They said it was truly innovative," he said.

"If I hear one more compliment about how my idea is good with no action to back it up, I swear—"

"Scarlet," he said, trying to calm me down, "please don't take it personally."

"Before I started this venture, all I could dream about was that one person, someone, *anyone,* would say something nice about my idea. But that's not enough," I said.

"But Scarlet," he said, "*I* care. I backed you up. I gave you what I could."

He reached for my hand. He was absolutely right. He had done everything he could for me and more. He'd certainly gone that extra mile. *Why am I shouting at him? None of this is his fault. It is just my frustration.* I remembered that and gave Roseword a big hug, thanking him for being there for me, for being the best investor one could ever hope for.

"Don't worry, kiddo," he said, suddenly brightening. "This isn't over by a long shot."

chapter 35

I was now a woman obsessed; I couldn't get the project out of my mind. I called Caroline and told her that I had the sequence I needed, that we were closer than ever to a prototype. She was very excited to hear it and said she would pass it along right away, as soon as we hung up, in fact. She told me a little bit about the dreadful meeting and was very discouraged about the fact that management would not take on the chick-sexing project. I asked her what she thought the problem was and, like Roseword, she said she had no clue. They were fighting to get this project into the sale agreement, and then suddenly backed out.

I asked her if, perhaps, the sequence would help give us some leverage, and she said she'd try. I told her that if, before, the technology was just in theory, it was now verified, and was very likely to be up and running soon with the right investment. I told her that I was disappointed because I felt I had put all my eggs in one basket in hopes that their injection machine would complement my method, and that together, we could do it. She agreed that I was right, and that she felt the same way.

I believed I had done the best I could have, since this project had a unique advantage that had now become a huge disadvantage. There were two or three companies to collaborate with and five potentially significant customers. This meant that we would only depend on a few people to be successful, so we wouldn't have to run from customer to customer to make a sale. If we could not depend on the injection companies, we did not have anyone to collaborate with, and we would need to either do it all on our own and develop an injection machine or give up the idea entirely.

I needed William, so I went to the pub on Tuesday. Predictably, there he was, sitting at the table with my cinnamon apple pie, waiting for me. What a pleasant sight. I was delighted to see him.

"How's my scientist this evening?"

"I'm a catastrophe," I said. "And you?"

"A little tired. I haven't been sleeping well," he said, but he didn't elaborate.

I told him our news about the meeting with RICPCom. He sympathized, and suggested that maybe I could continue with my other projects and reconsider the chick project. It was true that I did have other ideas to hang on to, but I was so emotionally invested in the chick project that I couldn't imagine letting it go. Then, when I confessed to him that I had called Caroline and told her about the sequence, he suddenly turned pale.

"I warned you specifically not to tell anyone, especially not Caroline," he said.

"But this might be our only chance," I cried.

I was shocked when, next, he got up, took my hand, and asked me to dance. We'd never done that before. We moved to a dark corner of the bar that doubled as a dance floor. He pulled me close and whispered into my ear. I felt like I might faint, though not because of the danger he was warning me of.

"I have reason to believe that by giving Caroline the information about the sequence, you put yourself in grave danger," he said. "I want us to finish this dance and get out of here and go somewhere private. We will go somewhere outside, where no one can hear us."

After the song ended, I followed him without saying another word. We walked outside, through the narrow streets and small alleyways, past buildings I had never seen in the city before. All I knew was that we were going west, in the direction of the sea. We reached the beach and walked for a half an hour on the sand, quickly, until we reached a secluded cave area beside a cliff.

"Let me check your purse," he said. "Please. They might be listening."

I gave it to him and he sorted through it, checking methodically for bugs. I trusted him, but he was acting a bit too strangely for my taste. If this was a trick to get me alone, I wasn't going to be happy.

I looked out at the sea and waited for him to finish searching. Eventually, I just got tired and laid my head on my jacket on the sand. He did the same, next to me.

"William," I said, whispering, "what is going on?"

"They don't want you to do this," he said, "and they'll go to great lengths to see that your work stops."

"But who?!" I asked.

He didn't answer. Instead, he put his hand on my face and pulled my hair back softly. Then he played with one of my curls.

"I am so sorry," he said, "I wish things could be different."

"William! You must tell me!"

"I don't think it's Caroline or RICPCom. I think she's on your side, like she claims," he said.

"Then who is it? Who is causing all this pain? Is it Cole?"

"Avian Industrial, Scarlet," he said. "It has to be."

The words felt like fire in my ears. "But we could save them so much money!" I said, my voice involuntarily rising above a whisper before William reached out to hush me. "Isn't that what all businesses want?"

"But that's just the thing, Scarlet. It won't save them money. It'll *cost* them."

I don't know if it was the beer or simply exhaustion, but I wasn't on my game. My head was fuzzy, and it felt like I couldn't follow what he was saying.

"Come again?"

"There's a proposed bill making its way up the chain in the capitol," he said. "Technologies categorized as 'green' will be mandatorily incorporated into existing businesses. If a technology exists that can give an industry access to cleantech, they *must* use it, or pay the price."

"So you're saying—"

"I am saying, Scarlet, that if your chick-sexing technology becomes accessible, the public has a right to demand its use—for the ethical reasons as well as the environmental reasons."

"So the general public is actually my customer!" I realized.

"Yep!" William smiled, a rare occurrence for this strange and serious night. "That is the good news. But the bad news is that it makes Avian your enemy rather than your ally."

I was furious. This was all about saving money—millions of dollars, yes, but it was chump change to a company that had revenues like Avian's.

"They'd rather not loose an extra cent and leave things as they are."

"Cheapskates," I spat. "I would do good things with that money."

"I know you would, sweet Scar."

He looked at me, leaned in closer, and kissed me on the nose. Then he leaned over and kissed my lips. His kiss tasted like, well, like sweet cinnamon apple pie. I did not want to hear any more that night. I just wanted to feel his arms around me.

William explained it all to me later. He said it was a near certainty that the law would pass, and that we had thrown a wrench in the works by involving two competing companies. Someone was bound to end up helping us develop the technology, and that's what kicked Avian into high gear. Caroline had naïvely been informing them of my progress all the while, as she had thought that it would make them want to buy RICPCom.

"They had to do something, Scarlet," William said. "These people don't like to lose from the bottom line."

"But taking Debauchee? Are they going to take out everyone who wants to develop a chick-sexing solution?"

"I wouldn't put it past them. That's why you're in danger," he said. "Now, about the sequence. You didn't write down anywhere, right?"

"No," I said. "I listened to you about that. It's only in my head."

"Very good, Scarlet. Now we just have to lie low for a while. Meanwhile, we also need to transfer your tubes to Joel, so that he can continue working on developing the prototype," he suggested.

"Is that a good idea? Will Joel be safe working on it?"

"It doesn't matter if it's a good idea, or a safe idea. It's the *only* idea. It's the only way to get you out of this. As long as they know you are alive and you have that sequence, you are a ticking time bomb. They have managed to gain control of the injection company indirectly, but you are on the loose. They underestimated you."

That may be the case, I thought. But every inch of me still trembled with fear.

William pulled me close.

"Everything will be fine, Scarlet. You can trust me."

He held me tightly, and we didn't say anything. The minutes ticked by. Then, suddenly, he spoke.

"I have a confession to make, Scarlet," he said.

I felt my heart clench like a fist. I couldn't handle any more bad news.

"Please, let it be something good," I said.

"Our meeting was not accidental. I mean, at the bar that first night."

"What do you mean?"

"Caroline phoned me shortly after your first call and asked me to keep an eye on you. You were right on the money: RICPCom was searching for any lead they could find on the chick-sexing method, and I was the person they wanted to help them get that lead," he said.

"So you're not who you said you are?" My heart was falling into a dark abyss. I could barely find the words.

"No, I *am*. I am a newsman and I do own a website. A few years back, I did an article on the injection machine and I met Caroline. We kept in touch. After you called, she asked me to meet you. I thought I might get an inside scoop, so I followed you to the bar that night."

"I thought you were on my side," I said, anger and sadness fighting for top billing in my heart.

"I am!" He grabbed my hand. "As soon as I met you and came to know you, I knew you really wanted to accomplish the chick-sexing. I told Caroline just that."

"You were a double agent? You told her everything I said!?" I cried.

"I was *their* agent at first," he said, "but I'm a single agent now. Yours, only yours, Scarlet. You're the one I want to protect. You're the one I want to be with."

"Against all odds?"

"Against all odds, my dear Scarlet," William said, and enveloped me in a warm kiss. The night, as horrible as it had been, turned out to be perfect after all.

chapter 36

I was ready to spring into action—or as ready as I'd ever be, now that I had a plan. The next morning, I made a call to my friend at the lab and told her I would not be into work today and that, in fact, I probably would be away for a few days.

"I need a favor," I told her.

"Anything," she said.

I gave her specific instructions. She was to open the fridge and take out the blue tube box on the second shelf from the bottom and put it in her bag and take it home with her. I asked her to put it in the fridge when she got home. The next morning, she was to take it to a mutual friend's home and leave it with him. I'd send Joel to pick it up from there. Finally, I asked her not to mention that she had spoken to me, especially if someone came to the lab and inquired about my absence.

William was coming out of the shower and came into the room wrapped in a towel to give me a kiss good morning. My heart thumped in my chest at the memory of our first night together.

"Joel will pick up the tubes tomorrow morning," I said to William, filling him in on the execution of our plan.

"Does that mean we have the rest of the day off?" he asked with his devilish smile.

"Pretty much," I said. "I think we've got to lie low today and hide out."

"That sounds like a perfect plan to me," he said. He moved closer and wrapped his strong arms around me. "In the meantime, you should just rest. We need to keep you safe."

I started to talk about all that needed to be done; Joel should set up another lab so that we could eventually get back to work. Without the daily routine of the lab, I felt like a fish out of water. But William was right. The stakes were too high for me right now, even if I was uncomfortable. *Well,* I thought as I looked into his eyes, *I'm not* totally *uncomfortable . . .*

"Safe sounds good to me, if you are nearby," I said. I crawled back into bed and waited for him, delirious with joy. When I finally let go of my need to be in the lab, spending the whole day in bed seemed like a dream come true. I could do this for a long time, I thought, or at least two or three weeks.

And so, while we waited, that's what we did, staying inside during the day and secreting out at night. We went skinny-dipping by the light of the moon at the beach. We spent a night out at the theater and took in *The Lion King*, although William joked that *Beauty and the Beast* would suit us better. We held each other close each night, and lulled ourselves to sleep sharing our secrets and hopes for the future. Pillow talk was my favorite.

"My dear Scarlet, I can't find the words to describe what I feel for you. And words are my job. Explaining how much I love you and why I love you would be like describing how water tastes; it's impossible. I love seeing you happy and my biggest reward is seeing you smile," he whispered in my ear.

"Aww, go on," I said, blushing to my bones.

"One word from you changes my whole mood. I only chat with you for a second, and it makes my day. One text or one call would set me free."

"But we never text, silly, we just meet at the pub."

"I know, that's why I am chained still. Unchain my heart!"

"You mean, unchain your phone number! Give it up! Oh! I forgot to ask: are you even single?"

"Yes, of course," he said, surprised that I would even suggest otherwise.

"Just checking," I said, smiling. "So, no kids either?"

"Scarlet, you have this incredible way of making my heart happy. My love for you will never end. My smile for you will never fade. I will love you always! I only want kids with you."

"You promise? Even when this whole mess is over, with the chicks and all?"

"I will love you as I have never loved another or ever will again. I love you with all that I am and all that I will ever be. The hardest thing I could ever do is to forget about you. I looked forward to seeing you every week and became attached to you. What more can a man say to the woman who opened her heart to him, allowing him to feel the warmth of her love across the distance that separates them?"

"You mean the distance of the length of the table that separated us in the pub each meeting!?" I asked, laughing. "I'm not trying to be sarcastic here, it's just that you always make me laugh." I lowered my eyes, listening to him quietly.

"I try to put my feelings into words, but I fail miserably. The feeling of both being scared and at peace with holding you, of having butterflies and a sense of calm."

"You do fail miserably, but it's so cute beyond words. I want to put you in a bun with some ketchup, mustard, and pickles and eat you up," I said. I laid my hand on his cheeks softly.

"I am serious, Scar, hear me out."

"Yes, of course, go on, I am writing this down. You will sign at the bottom." I pretended to text on my iPhone. I didn't know what to do with myself in the midst of his declaration.

"My dear, I never thought I had the capacity to love anybody as much as I love you now. Yet my love continues to mature, growing beyond the realm of my heart. It seems that you have become the fiber of my soul, the very reason for my existence. I prayed so long to find someone like you." He suddenly had such a serious expression on his face.

"Yes, we never like to think of failure, but it's manageable if you are loved, if you have a safety net."

"A love so passionate as yours, I could never dream to find and you brought peace to my aching, cold, empty heart," he said, and held me close. "I love you unconditionally."

Tears began to run down my face.

If I tried hard enough, it was almost like I could forget that we were in hiding, that if anyone knew where I was, I would be in danger. Instead, it felt like we were on vacation. It was heaven, somehow, even in the midst of the hell we were in.

Todd called me every day to update me on a secure line that William had arranged. We also used a special code that William had developed and installed on my laptop, so that we were able to e-mail back and forth with some confidence that nothing was getting passed on to the wrong hands. Joel also communicated with us, telling us about the work that was progressing on a daily basis, even while I was hiding away. Todd, though he wasn't naïve, was still flabbergasted by the dangerous developments. He said he'd learned a valuable lesson, and would never underestimate what money and corporate interests could do. I told him not to be so hard on himself, that there was no way we could have predicted this turn of events. I think I was trying to convince myself as much as I was trying to assuage his guilt.

My friend, Bob, the property manager, had given me many sets of keys to apartments all over the city, and we kept relocating our safe house every so often. I was so much in love with William during those weeks we spent together, moving under the cover of night. It was also the first time I had felt so loved in return, even though, at times, he still felt distant and unknowable to me.

One night, our little nest was in a building on the bad side of town; the apartment was worn down and the paint was peeling from the walls. The oven didn't work and there was no balcony to overlook the beautiful city lights. But something about it reminded me of home—something about the simplicity of it. Since I hadn't been home in a while, I became a little melancholy, and William could tell. He helpfully suggested that we try to find a local pub, perhaps one with some decent pie. That put a smile on my face. We went downstairs and walked through an alley, avoiding piles of garbage and trying to hide our faces from the light in the event that we were being followed. Suddenly, I heard a noise, and when I turned around, we saw two men running toward us. William grabbed my hand and we sprinted down the alley, eventually turning into an old, vacant building.

I gagged on the strong smell of urine that permeated the air. William, still holding onto my hand tightly, pulled me under an old bed, its rusty springs sagging onto the floor. I caught myself thinking about when I'd had my last tetanus shot. We hid underneath the bed as the sound of heavy boots entered the room, walking around and eventually being silenced by a much worse sound: a gunshot. I covered my mouth as we waited.

When the danger seemed to have passed, we scurried out from under the bed and went through the building's back door, which connected directly into a dance club. Hiding ourselves in the throng of bodies, we shouted into each other's ears to be heard above the thumping bass line.

"That was close," William said, pulling me near. He shouted that he had gotten a glimpse of the men. One was younger, the one with the heavy boots. He had a tattoo of two hearts pierced by an arrow on his upper right arm. The other was older, about two hundred pounds, with shiny white shoes. He was the one holding the gun. When we were reasonably sure that we were safe and hadn't been followed into the club, we slid off to a corner booth to gather ourselves. Part of me didn't care if they shot me right there; I would die happy and in love.

"This is getting bad," William said, trying to crack a smile.

"It's not so bad," I said, trying to keep the mood light although I was shaken up, too. "You'll take care of me, and we can go anywhere in the world with Roseword's help. Plus, Bob probably has some apartments in other countries too."

He held my hand and we sat in silence for a while.

"May I have this dance?" I asked, and we did, the nightmare fading into a dream.

The next morning we woke up, packed our bags and took a bus down south. We talked and talked, discussing our past and our future, trying to avoid the delicate subject of our present. We talked about kids. He wanted six, and right away. I smiled and marveled at the mess I'd gotten myself into.

At the bus station, the men hawking vacation-apartment rentals were easy to find. We rented a room by the beachfront, on an upper floor, so we could look down below us and see the lay of the land. We felt a little safer, but we knew not to take that for granted; who knew what tomorrow would bring. They could easily be on our tail, whomever they were.

"You know, I could always go back to working on my other projects," I said to William, perhaps foolishly. "Without the secret sequence, the method is still a general method for detecting species by the differences in their DNA. The sequence is what makes it unique and solvable for the chickens. There could be other applications."

"Yes, but we talked about that, Scarlet. You *could* have done that, if only they did not know you had the sequence. Once you had that sequence, they became threatened. You could apply the solution to their industry at any time," said William.

Just then, someone blew a tire outside. I screamed and jumped. William told me to get down, and after looking outside and seeing nothing, he came back in to calm me.

"Maybe we should get a pistol, so we can protect ourselves," I said.

I was surprised when he shook his head.

"If we kill those two guys, they will just send more," he said. "We need to solve this intellectually."

"If you say so, but I think a gal has a right to protect herself from the bad guys," I replied.

We spent our days in hiding and our nights on the beach, sitting on the sand and dreaming of a future we both weren't sure we'd be able to have. In the meantime, Roseword was contacting people he knew at the Department of Environment and Natural Resources. He was pulling every connection he had to get us back on track. He now wanted this chick-sorting application to work more than ever—and we wanted to come back home and be safe.

Remarkably, he found a lead, in his own backyard, no less. It turned out that after Roseword had learned that Cole was snooping around in my lab that day he called, he had become suspicious of Cole.

He called us to explain that he'd never confided in Cole about anything which related to Spells. He'd then had him followed and saw him meeting with Mr. Zohar Zoffer, the CEO of Avian Industrial. He had checked Cole's home and his computer, as well as tapped his phone, and all the data confirmed that Cole was working for Zoffer all along to undermine Spells. Roseword had turned all the data over to the police and it was now under investigation.

He suspected Cole gained access to all my data through Roseword's computer in the office, but the one thing he was missing was my secret sequence. He had been attempting to fish out whether I had gotten it or not when he came into the lab that day, which had set him up to get caught. He had been trying to intimidate me into confessing what I had.

Roseword said that, most likely, he was getting paid by Zoffer as well as working for Roseword's VC as head of operations. But the interesting thing was that his sharp inner conflict between attraction to scientific progress and his greed for money had led him to divide his loyalty between us and Zoffer. He hadn't told Zoffer about the trade-secret sequence, fortunately, but he may have been the reason for the disappearance of Debauchee. Who knows if, perhaps, he had wanted access to the trade secret for his own personal profit? He wasn't in custody yet; he was still a free man.

William and I were pretty shaken up by Roseword's news. I asked him if we should look into traveling abroad. He said they probably had people everywhere, but nevertheless, he arranged with Roseword for us to get out of the country for a while—just us and our passports. We knew we'd find what we needed when we got there.

We landed in beautiful weather in a small airport in Italy, where the sun warmed our faces on the tarmac. We rented a little hideaway in the forest, among the lakes, still trying to enjoy our time together despite the danger and uncertainty that might lie ahead.

One day, we even tried to go mushroom hunting, but couldn't find any of the mushrooms that we were searching for. It turned out William liked to go mushroom hunting as a kid, and I found that rather funny. Why would you *hunt* a mushroom? But he liked eating mushrooms and pickling mushrooms, and had studied for quite some time to become an expert mushroom hunter. I joked with him that I was trying to be very quiet so the mushrooms wouldn't escape. He didn't find that funny.

After hunting around for a while, we bathed in the lake. It was freezing, but I gave it a try and screamed "NO!" all the way in. Swimming was fun once I'd warmed up a little. We had the place all to ourselves, too, and I caught myself appreciating the Natural Beauty we'd found. Suddenly, in the midst of all that, an idea sparked.

That night, I called Joel and asked him to set aside the chicken samples and take bacteria instead. I asked him to use the method we developed to recognize the DNA of the bacteria, thus detecting a specific kind of bacteria in low quantities. He had to use our protocol but find a sequence that would match the bacteria.

"What are you cooking up now, Scarlet?" asked William. "Why are you changing it from chickens? I thought Roseword wanted you to try and reach a prototype as soon as possible so that we can show the world that the technology is accessible and win the game. Then we would be safe from Avian. They'd have no choice once we'd gone public."

"It'll take us a year at least, William," I said. "And not only do I want to stop running for my life, I want to be a part of the science! I don't want to have to hide away while others get the glory."

"So what do you suggest?" asked William, surprised.

"You'll see," I said with a coy smile. "If this works out, I'll know what to do."

He was quiet for a moment, thinking it over.

"Well," he said, "since I can't do anything to help, in the meantime, would you read me this book?"

I smiled and said I'd be happy to do it. William loved it when I read to him, and he especially liked it when I made up stories before going to bed. After I read to him for a while, we made grand plans to go forage for more mushrooms in the future. William explained how we could dry and pickle them, and that was enough to put me to sleep for the night.

We waited a few days until we heard back from Joel. He had begun on the experiments as I asked, focusing on the common bacteria *E. coli*.

Since there are different strains of *E. coli,* it is important to be able to differentiate between the different strains to prevent disease. I found a paper that described repetitive sequences of DNA, which help differentiate between the strains. I sent these sequences to Joel and asked him to check our method on these strains to identify the difference between them. The paper I read was phenomenal; it described sequences of DNA in the bacteria, which were used by the bacteria to fight incoming viruses. We could use these sequences to differentiate between different strains of bacteria.

Joel was working to see if our method would work on differentiating the bacteria, and said he was a few weeks away from a result. I called Todd and told him he needed to prepare a presentation that incorporated our bacteria research in place of the chickens, asking him to show the economic value of using it against pathogens in the biodefense industry.

I hate to say it, but after I had hatched the plan, I went straight back to spending my time with William relatively carefree. It was almost like our honeymoon.

We spent the next few weeks traveling in Italy and drove through Tuscany. Florence was beautiful and the narrow streets made me feel comfortable. It was busy with all the locals and tourists. We went to see the art at the Uffizi Gallery, which was beyond words. We stayed at a villa outside of Florence and traveled somewhere new every day. In Pisa we visited a professor I knew well from my undergraduate days. He had a lab nearby and was happy to see us. He took us to the best coffee shop in town and explained that in Italy, one does not drink espresso after eleven o'clock in the morning.

Later that day I asked the professor if it would be possible for me to work in his lab for a couple of weeks. He said it would not be a problem, and that he would have a bench ready for me the next day. I was thrilled to work in a lab in Tuscany; the location was the most inspiring one I'd found yet. I called Joel and asked him to give me the details for the protocol he was working on. He had made a lot of progress and was almost finished. I ordered some things that took a few days to arrive and then got to work. The other students in the lab were nice and extremely welcoming.

William warned me that it would not be safe to work there for more than a couple of weeks, and that I may be putting the lab in danger. Then, we got the call from Roseword, he stated plainly that Cole had been found dead in his $5 million house. He didn't offer any more details and sounded in shock and saddened. I offered my condolences. That day I learned a life lesson better than any other: indeed, some things are better left unsaid.

I kept all this in the back of my mind and continued ahead with my research as if I were being chased, pushing forward as much as possible each day until I reached my breakthrough. One afternoon, it all clicked: things were working perfectly. I came home to our villa to tell William that we should pack and get going; we had a week to return straight into the lion's den.

I asked him where he wanted to travel and what he wanted to see before we went back.

He answered, "The only place I want to be is in this villa, and I only want to see your eyes."

It didn't take much convincing.

The day finally came when we needed to return. We hadn't seen those two men ever again, but we knew better than to relax and stop looking over our shoulders. We continued to pay only in cash, concealing our real identities from all whom we met.

I called Joel and told him to pack up the bacteria, tubes, and other things we needed for a demonstration and asked Caroline to set up a meeting with the head of Avian Industrial, Zoffer, at a hotel close to where he lived. She knew him personally, and when I told her it was imperative that we meet with him directly, she agreed.

I called Roseword and asked him to make the arrangements to meet us at the hotel and to arrange a conference room where we could all talk in private. He said that would be no problem, but asked if I was positively sure I knew what I was doing.

"Positively sure, Scarlet?" he asked again after I hesitated.

"I'm positively sure that I hope so," I said with a weak chuckle.

William asked me the same question, and though I gave him the same answer, I still didn't elaborate on what exactly I had in mind. I could trust no one at this point. It was my work, my career, my life hanging on the line—and no one else's. All the risk was on me.

We were at the hotel near the meeting site, and I was praying that we would not get killed before I'd had my chance to say what I'd come to say. *Who knows?* I thought, after what they'd done to Mr. Debauchee. Actually, I wasn't even sure *what* they had done to him; I just knew that he hadn't been heard from since his disappearance.

Todd came by to see us and I was delighted to see him. He, too, asked me if I was sure about this meeting and I reassured him that I needed this and it would go over fine. He asked me what it was about, but I told him I could not tell him and that he would find out soon enough.

When we walked into the conference room, Caroline was there, standing next to a severe-looking man in an intimidating black suit.

"Meet Zohar Zoffer," she said, introducing us to the CEO of Avian Industrial—and, very likely, the man who had put our lives in such grave danger.

I tried to pull of my best acting job yet.

"It's very nice to meet you," I said, looking around warily and watching as Joel set everything up.

Roseword was there already, sitting at the corner of the table and smiling at me. I had not seen him for so long, and I was relieved that he had come.

"Since we are all here, I suggest we get started," I began, summoning up a well of strength from God knows where.

Zoffer nodded, and everyone took a seat.

"Mr. Zoffer, this might surprise you, but we're actually not here to talk about the poultry business. Rather, we're here to gauge your interest in a product we've been developing, one that can detect DNA in small quantities. We believe that a prominent businessman like yourself will appreciate a first look at our innovative technology."

He looked slightly suspicious of us, but hadn't shut me down yet. So I continued.

"We are now going to demonstrate to you a method for detecting bacteria in low copy numbers. This can be used for different purposes, mainly to detect pathogens, early on, before they cause great damage," I looked to Joel and asked him to set up the reaction.

"We have here five petri dishes, each containing a different strain of bacteria, as noted on the back of each dish."

I asked Zoffer to choose one, which he did, and then I picked it up and showed the back of it to everyone except myself and Joel.

"I will pick up a clone of the bacteria and set it in this tube. In a few minutes, we will read the tube in the machine and we will be able to determine which strain of bacteria this is."

We waited a few minutes and Joel read the results: *E. coli* strain K12. I turned the plate that was chosen upside down and asked Zoffer to read aloud what it said. It was indeed *E. coli* strain K12.

"We can try this again later with the other plates, if you wish, but as you just saw, this was a blind test in which you chose the plate without us seeing the name. But I am sure you realize that this is no trick, no sleight of hand. Plain and simple, it works. Now, before we go on, Todd has prepared a presentation to show us the attributes of the technology, including patent-pending material for you to see," I said.

Once Todd finished presenting, I stood up and began to speak again.

"Mr. Zoffer, we have shown you that our technology, according to the new laws, is accessible as certified green, due to its reduction of waste in the incubators. This, as you know, means your company will be required to apply it, along with all the regulations, reports and taxes involved. This can get very expensive indeed and lots of paper pushing involved. However, as it stands now, it cannot be used within the poultry industry in the incubators within the hatcheries. As the CEO of Avian Industrial, it's pretty much useless to you for detecting bacteria, I'd imagine. It seems that it is useful as a general method, which suits different applications and demands of detecting DNA."

"So why bring me here?" asked Zoffer, his irritation radiating from his pinched face.

"Mr. Roseword has taken a good look at the new law, Mr. Zoffer," I continued carefully. "It states that if a green technology exists, and if that technology is general and is not intended for a specific application, it may be sold and bought as a regular business deal. If a technology is general and is later adopted for a specific green application, it falls under the radar and cannot be forced upon the receiving company. Green-technology rules apply only when there is a solution to a specific waste problem such as chick-sexing."

"Such as the chick-sexing. That's a solution to a problem, huh?" he retorted.

"Not if the solution is general, which it is, in this case. Let me remind you that you just witnessed the possible application for bacteria detection," I said.

"I'm not sure I understand what you're getting at," he said, and I felt pleased that we'd cracked his calm demeanor.

"Let's just say, Mr. Zoffer, that if you've thought you could not charge for it, but just had to pay for it, this is not the case. You *can* install it and still charge for it, since it is a general solution, which your company is adopting," said Roseword, who got my drift. Caroline smiled.

"But if it is only a general solution and useless to the poultry industry, how am I going to buy it, install it, and adopt or even charge for it?" Zoffer said, his voice rising in pitch with irritation.

"The secret sequence! We have a *key* to activate the technology; once you have it, it turns from useless to beneficial to the poultry industry," I said.

"Like turning the pumpkin into Cinderella's carriage," said William.

"Now, if you have your own key, your own sequence, which you have developed, then you do not need to acquire it from us, and thus it is yours to use as you please," I continued.

"The new law says that a corporation may charge for its self-developed products, even if they have a Green Seal. That is in order to encourage big corporations to develop their own green solutions," added Roseword.

"So if, let's say, I had the sequence, that my company developed, we could use this for chick-sexing and I could make a profit on the green eggs and not end up taking on the whole expense of it alone?" asked Zoffer.

"Exactly," said Todd, grinning.

"And if you buy the general technology from us, or license it, somehow, in some way, I can assure you, you will end up with the secret sequence in your hands," I said. "I'll guarantee it."

All of the air had been sucked out of the room as we waited for Zoffer to contemplate the deal. We knew we were making a deal with the devil, but if it worked, we could go back to our lives and live in peace. I understood that in business, as in life, compromise is the better option and everybody wins!

Finally, he spoke: "I think you have yourself a deal, young lady," he said, extending his hand to shake mine.

Before I clasped his hand, I said, "And part of that deal is that I get my privacy back."

"Now all that is left to do is settle on a price," Todd said. He turned his head to Lauralynn who had just entered the room. She was late for our meeting, but, as usual, had perfect timing.

I smiled at my William, knowing that we'd positioned things such that Zoffer would pay top dollar for the technology. But what I had really walked away with was priceless: my life, my freedom and my passion . . . all intact.

Later that evening William and I took a stroll as he kept teasing me about the sale and kissing me. "Luckily you kept that secret sequence to yourself," said William.

Before we went to sleep that night, I asked him about the future. He said he wanted six kids with me. I told him that now that I was going to work for the Poultry Corp., I would need to move away. I expected him to say that he would move away with me and follow me anywhere in the world. After all, he did work from home and home is where the heart is. Me being the helpless romantic.

Instead, he said we would work it out and that I could visit him on the first and third weekend of every month and he could visit me on the second and fourth. Yes, that is how he wants to build a relationship with trust and intimacy, via email and occasional weekends. He insisted that he needed my attention, but I needed more from him. I knew it was not going to be every weekend. We will be lucky if it is twice a year with our busy schedules.

"William," I said, kissing him on the cheek and the tip of his nose, "are you going to email me those six kids?" I always knew in my heart, he was and always will be, a double agent. Not to be trusted with the secret sequence. He could never be wholly mine.

Printed in the USA
CPSIA information can be obtained
at www.ICGtesting.com
JSHW022334140824
68134JS00019B/1470

9 781683 504641